"He is the most specific of writers; at any given moment, we know precisely what year it is, how old the characters are and even the exact address of the action. Sometimes those coordinates are in Palm Springs or Beverly Hills, but more often Schwartz hums a love song to New York: the Central Park carousel, Sardi's, Fifth Avenue, the FDR Drive . . . Schwartz will make you laugh . . . pull at your heartstrings."
                                        —*Newsweek*

"An absorbing . . . moving . . . bittersweet story." —*Los Angeles Times*

"Captures the ineffable sadness of lost time . . . in his portrayal of the past as an abiding presence, Jonathan Schwartz excels."
                        —*The New York Times Book Review*

JONATHAN SCHWARTZ has enjoyed fame as both a singer and as a pop-music disc jockey on New York's WNEW. He has also won renown as a writer for such publications as *The Atlantic, Harper's, Esquire,* and *The Paris Review,* and as author of two previous books, *Almost Home* and *Distant Stations.* He lives in New York with his wife and son.

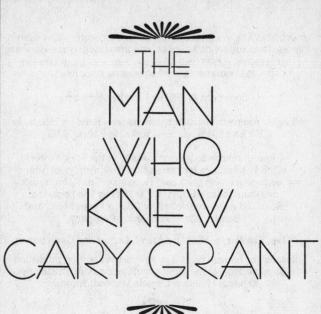

THE MAN WHO KNEW CARY GRANT

A NOVEL BY JONATHAN SCHWARTZ

A PLUME BOOK

NEW AMERICAN LIBRARY

A DIVISION OF PENGUIN BOOKS USA INC., NEW YORK
PUBLISHED IN CANADA BY
PENGUIN BOOKS CANADA LIMITED, MARKHAM, ONTARIO

Copyright © 1988 by Jonathan Schwartz

Grateful acknowledgment is made to the Song Writer's
Guild of America for permission to reprint lyrics from
"Swinging Down the Lane" (words by Gus Kahn, music
by Isham Jones). Copyright © 1923 by Leo Feist, Inc.
Renewed rights controlled by Gilbert Keyes Music and
Bantam Music Publishing Company.

"Over The Purple Hills" by Alan J. Lerner and Carly Simon

This is an authorized reprint of a hardcover edition published by
Random House, Inc., and simultaneously in Canada by
Random House of Canada Limited, Toronto.

PLUME TRADEMARK REG. U.S. PAT. OFF. AND FOREIGN COUNTRIES
REGISTERED TRADEMARK—MARCA REGISTRADA
HECHO EN BRATTLEBORO, VT., U.S.A.

SIGNET, SIGNET CLASSIC, MENTOR, ONYX, PLUME,
MERIDIAN and NAL BOOKS are published *in the United States by*
New American Library, a division of Penguin Books USA Inc.,
1633 Broadway, New York, New York 10019, *in Canada* by
Penguin Books Canada Limited, 2801 John Street,
Markham, Ontario L3R 1B4

LIBRARY OF CONGRESS CATALOGING-IN-PUBLICATION DATA
Schwartz, Jonathan, 1938-
The man who knew Cary Grant / Jonathan Schwartz.
p.   cm.
Reprint. Originally published: New York : Random House, c1988
ISBN 0-452-26310-7
I. Title.
PS3569.C566M3   1989
813'.54—dc20   89-8677
CIP

First Plume Printing, October, 1989

1   2   3   4   5   6   7   8   9

PRINTED IN THE UNITED STATES OF AMERICA

For
Ellie Renfield
Daphne Merkin
Sam Vaughan

CONTENTS

THE
MAN
WHO
KNEW
CARY GRANT

Norman Savitt wrote the melodies first, then the lyrics. He worked in a high-ceilinged studio in the Carnegie Hall building. He often slept there, on a Castro. He had acquired the stage rights to the film *Roman Holiday*, but work had slowed to a trickle. As a composer-lyricist, he needed the libretto, at least the first act. It was being written by a woman in the San Fernando Valley who refused to come to New York "until it's absolute critical drop dead essential." Weeks went by with no word from the West. Norman stayed more and more in the studio, sending out to the Stage Deli for meals, lying on the foldout holding a portable radio on his chest, listening to the news repeat itself. He became an expert on the moon walk and Chappaquiddick. He brooded over his own calamity: no money raised, no libretto, no theater, no leading man or woman. Ten years of not being able to get shows on, of other people dragging their feet, indecision piled upon indecision, money pledged and then pulled away. And again, with a great property like *Roman Holiday*, there was nothing to do but lie in bed with the radio on. Norman, who lived on Fifth Avenue, went home now and then, though the Carnegie studio suited him better. He could shut out the light by closing the heavy gray curtains, creating gloom.

"He's in my gut," he told his son, Jesse. "The man with the pitchfork."

The man with the pitchfork's real name was colitis, a word never spoken by Norman. "He just comes and goes," Norman often said. "He's got comp house seats anytime he wants."

Jesse's mother, who had died seventeen years earlier, had frequently told her son, "Your father is the most vital man I've ever known." Meaning out there, part of it, eloquent, social, informed, stubborn, brilliant, part of it, alive alive alive.

Norman had never remarried, though he took women to the theater and spoke with women on the phone.

He spoke to Jesse every day. Jesse would stop by the studio and sit at the foot of the bed. They would talk above the news in the room's dim light. Jesse, who had turned thirty-one over the summer, brought his father borscht when told of visits from the man with the pitchfork. The man with the pitchfork liked borscht. Jesse imagined him flooded by it, a cartoon character bobbing in a pink sea.

"Very tasty," Norman would say, drinking his glass of borscht in bed.

In his own apartment in the Village, Jesse's girlfriend, Amy, made him chicken pot pie.

"Very tasty," Jesse said, at meal's end, on his way to bed so that he could listen to the radio before going off to sleep.

"Why don't you take your father on a vacation?" Amy said to Jesse, crawling into bed next to him.

Jesse hated being asked questions as he was falling asleep. Amy always had many questions ready for that time of day. Now Jesse regretted having mentioned Norman while eating the chicken pot pie.

"How about an exploratory trip to Nam," Jesse said. "Tunesmith Norman Savitt wants to *know*."

"You're a wise guy," Amy said.

The next day, sitting at the foot of the bed, Jesse said: "Let's take a drive tomorrow. Get out of the city."

"I'm not feeling my best," Norman said gravely.

"Doesn't matter. I'll rent a car. Would you like Amy to come?"

"You two go off together," Norman said.

"Daddy, you're not a weakling. Come on now, let's get out of this room. This Dickensian room. You *like* Amy. You told me she cheers you up."

"Oh but she does, she does. She's a very lovely girl."

"Maybe we'll have lunch in Bridgehampton, and a walk on the beach. The crowds are gone, it's October, how about it?"

"Let's see how I feel in the morning," Norman said.

"Amy's gotta know. *I've* gotta know."

"But you're not working. You have no schedule," Norman said.

"We realize that. We *all* realize I'm out of work," Jesse said angrily.

"I didn't mean anything by it," Norman said.

"I'm sure."

"Don't get sarcastic with me," Norman said.

"I could ask the same thing of you."

"I don't see how," Norman said.

———

JESSE RENTED FROM Avis.

Norman chose slacks and a turtleneck.

Jesse, double-parked, smiled at the sight of his father walking out of his apartment building on Fifth Avenue. The flair was back, restored from so long ago, from Jesse's childhood, from the days of the theater: Norman Savitt strolling down the avenue, meeting people he knew, stopping to talk, Jesse at his side. Nizer the lawyer, Lyons the columnist, Arlen the songwriter, Cary Grant. A crowd gathered around Grant and Norman and Jesse. "I'll bet you sing better than you think you do," Norman had said to Cary Grant. When they parted, a portion of the crowd followed Norman and Jesse. "Why are you following us?" Norman said to two women who must have been sisters. "Because if you know Cary Grant, you must *be* somebody," one of the women replied.

On this Thursday morning Norman looked to Jesse like a man who knew Cary Grant. A man in his mid-fifties perhaps, certainly not the sixty-eight that spelled the truth. Did Norman have a tan? Not possible, of course, what with the Carnegie curtains playing so large a role. But, still, a ruddiness, the solid suggestion of health—the man with the pitchfork off for the day, no borscht on this day, no relentless radio news.

Norman wore a tweed jacket over his turtleneck, an autumnal father on an outing.

"I want you to drive slowly, I want you to drive carefully," Norman said from the backseat.

"Jesse knows what he's doing in a car," Amy said, sitting next to Jesse in the front.

Jesse tried to remember if he had driven Amy anywhere in the year they had been together. One time, from Larchmont to the city in Amy's father's car, the morning after they first made love in Amy's father's empty house. They had shared a bottle of Dom Perignon in the car that morning, heading into town, hitting the West Side Highway in top spirits. Jesse had known what he was doing in a car.

"I haven't been to the Hamptons in years. One trip, your mother and I rented a limo to Quogue to see Bert and Anne." Norman said. "Friends of ours," he added for Amy, who had turned, facing him from the front.

"It was a gay day," he continued. "Your mother was feeling wonderful. Full of pep."

When full of pep, Carol had been much like her son. Though bedridden in a room as dark as the Carnegie studio, she remained challenging, her appetites raging: for books and music, and food, though she was restricted on this count. And jokes and laughter and questions. Norman had been sent out into the world to display the family's enthusiam, but from the corner room down the hall Carol had energized the whole show. Jesse wondered if his father's closed curtains were meant to fly at half-mast. He felt that the two of them would never be close enough to support such an inquiry.

"Jesse says she was sick," Amy said.

My mother was sick and she died in 1952. That was what Jesse had said, withholding information from someone he saw as provisional. Amy the painter. Paint on her elbows, a delicate girl with long red hair, a girl from Amherst, twenty-two years old: file her vote for the Youngbloods, vegetarian restaurants just east of the Fillmore, dancing, all kinds of dancing—the girl could rhumba, the girl could waltz, the girl could boogie, her long red hair flowing, her head thrown back, filled with marijuana jumble and Creedence Clearwater.

"Did he tell you how remarkable she was?" Norman asked.

"In his way," Amy said.

7

"Amy knows the story," Jesse said, irritated at them.

"Well, she *was* remarkable," Norman said.

"Yes," Amy said.

"People loved her," Norman said.

"Yes," Amy said.

"I remember once we were in Boston. Did I ever tell you this, Jesse?"

Norman really wanted to know if he had told Jesse this story. Norman had developed into quite a raconteur, haunting the past for each delightful piece of theater, his stories populated by Katharine Cornell and Max Gordon and Ira Gershwin. Now, at sixty-eight, Norman allowed them to tumble out as news, first time around. Occasionally he'd ask: Have I told you this? Usually when a third party was about, taking himself off the hook. Alone with Jesse, he'd start right up.

"Yes, but go on," Jesse said, had said many times.

"Well. We were in Boston, checking into the Ritz with a show—I forget which one—and we met Oscar Hammerstein in the lobby checking out. He'd been there for three weeks with a show of his own, and he was heading back to New York. Your mother asked him what room he'd had. It turned out it was the very room we were assigned. Oscar said to your mother: 'Carol, take a good look at the lamp by the desk.' Your mother asked why, and Oscar said: 'Because it's made of my skin.' "

"What did he mean?" Amy asked.

"He meant that he had just worked really hard," Jesse said.

"Uh-*huh,*" Amy said with appreciation. "He's a kind of legendary man, isn't he. I've never thought about what he must be like."

"He's dead," Jesse said.

8

"He was a *wonderful* legendary man," Norman said. "He was very warm. Everybody loved Oscar."

Jesse was pleased that his father had been kind enough to pick up on Amy's word "legendary" to keep her in the game. But the truth was probably that Norman had just run with it, picking up "legendary" from the sky, with no thought of Amy. If this was true, it didn't make him a villain, but it tempered Jesse's pleasure.

"Did he write *The Sound Of Music*?" Amy asked.

"Yes," Jesse snapped, trying to stop her.

"I loved *The Sound Of Music*," Amy said, oblivious.

"Did you," Norman said, showing, through the rearview mirror, what Jesse felt to be false interest.

"All those beautiful tunes," Amy said.

"It was Rodgers. Hammerstein wrote the words," Jesse said.

"I wonder what it's like going through life linked to somebody else like that," Amy said. "You're not just you, you're Hammerstein and *Rodgers*. All the work you do is under two names. I guess relationships can get real complicated."

Jesse wondered if his father found Amy alluring, or even erotic. What was the status of Norman's sexuality these days? Who, if anyone, came back to Fifth Avenue with him? What did they accomplish, once ensconced. Was the volume of his lust turned low because of the lack of progress in his work? Because of being sixty-eight? Only recently had Jesse been able to even consider his father's sexual tempo. It had always been difficult to imagine Norman Savitt posed in bed, lurching luridly in the comic posture of copulation. But in the last year or so, Jesse had forced himself to address the question. He wished to encounter his father in his mind without the curtains drawn.

"I guess songs like *they* wrote—Hammerstein and Rodgers—have become a little out-of-date, because of rock," Amy said, failing to relate Norman to their decline.

"Everything has sunk to the lowest possible level," Norman said, shaking his head in agreement. "There's no room anymore for the kind of quality that the theater once upon a time possessed. It was *made* of quality. Quality of the imagination."

"Well, I like rock," Amy said, "but I'll take Hammerstein and Rodgers. You know what I mean?" Amy encompassed Jesse the driver with a sweep of her arm.

"It's more complicated than that," Jesse said, once again irritated with everyone.

"What's so complicated?" Norman said. "Rock and roll has killed beautiful music. It's that simple. It's *that* simple."

Jesse and Norman had thrashed this one about before.

JESSE: It's changing times, unexpected influences, instrument amplification, we're not living in 1940, what about Hendrix, the Stones, Dylan—

NORMAN: I can't listen to that crap. It's just crap, is all it is. It's that simple.

JESSE: All of it isn't crap. Why is it so popular?

NORMAN: Because it's for punks, and the world is filled with punks. And they buy the records. And the networks own the record companies and the radio stations, and the radio stations play that crap, and it just shuts quality music out. It's that simple.

"Maybe it's just a cycle," Amy said cheerfully.

"I think I'm more cynical than you are," Norman said.

Jesse thought that his father's use of "cynical" suggested a real conversation with Amy, an earnest exchange of misinformation. They might just be able to go on with it all the way out to Bridgehampton: The Stones blah blah blah, networks blah blah blah, melody, crap, I'm more blah blah blah than you are, it's that simple.

"I'm not really cynical," Amy said, after thinking it over.

"You don't need cynicism, no one does," Norman said. "As a matter of fact, I think you're a very positive person."

"Thank you," Amy said.

"I didn't mean to demean your music," Norman said.

"Oh no," Amy said. "It's not my music. I like it all. Hammerstein and Rodgers, like I said."

"They wouldn't have much of a chance today. That's what I'm up against."

"There's always room for wonderful songs," Amy said.

"Time is running out," Norman replied softly.

"LET'S PULL OVER at the Green Thumb," Jesse said. "It's a great place. They have the best tomatoes in the world, especially now, before the first frost."

Jesse turned off the road and stopped the car in front of a roadside shop brimming with red and yellow tomatoes, and corn and zucchini and string beans and cabbage. The large tomatoes, resembling brain tumors, rode round and round on a large lazy Susan.

"The pick of the season," Jesse said, holding one of them up for his father.

Amy loved the flowers, the chrysanthemums and lilies and daisy pompons.

"This is charming," Norman said. "This is the perfect place for your mother," he told Jesse as he picked an enormous tomato from the slowly revolving display.

The only other customer in the shop was an attractive

woman somewhat younger than Jesse's father. She approached them with a smile.

"Norman," she said.

Jesse recognized her immediately. His father embraced her.

"And Jesse," she said.

Jesse was flooded by Lois Hayes, his mother's confidante, a regal and beautiful woman, generous to Jesse years ago, a foot-rubbing, story-telling visitor to the house, the wife of Norman's lawyer. She always came with her arms filled: with baskets of flowers and tins of chocolate and stacks of magazines and records for Jesse. She came and she stayed. She gossiped with Carol, she played gin rummy with Jesse, she prepared lunches right out of the air; they ate at the dining room table, sun streaming in through Venetian blinds: salads and squash pudding and wild rice and slivers of veal and velvet mashed potatoes and vegetable soup from scratch, and cherrystone clams in their shells that gleamed like gold in drops of lemon. Her husband had died a year after Carol. She had drifted away from the family after a year or so of occasional phone calls or a postcard from here or there: from Rio, from San Francisco, from Paris, even a postcard from New York showing the Empire State Building. At fourteen, Jesse knew that the New York postcard concluded Lois Hayes. He reasoned that there was now no distance that had to be traversed by her casually scribbled and uncommitted words; she was lost somewhere down the avenue that ran outside his very door.

Standing by the tomatoes in the Green Thumb, Jesse thought of that postcard, as he often had when catching a glimpse of the Empire State Building. "Good-bye," he had often said under his breath, until it had become an automatic response to the sight of the building. Time had blurred Lois

Hayes, leaving a disappearing good-bye in Jesse's heart, like the last moments of skywriting.

They caught up with each other among the lilies and the basil.

Lois Hayes was married to another lawyer—"Would you believe it?" she said.

They owned a house in Wainscott and rented an apartment on Central Park West. Her married name was Allenson, her husband's name was Dan.

She said she often thought of Norman and Jesse. She said she hadn't wanted to intrude on their lives without Carol, and then, somehow, time got out of hand. She wanted to know how they were, what they were doing. She was told that Norman was writing a show, and that Jesse was a freelance journalist. Jesse's girlfriend was Amy and she was over by the corn. She was told by both Norman and Jesse that she looked "stunning" and "youthful" and "just plain terrific."

Which was true, Jesse thought, as he listened to his father's compliments.

Lois Hayes had short blond hair and green eyes that were filled with the generosity Jesse recalled.

And that voice. It rolled back into Jesse like her warm vegetable soup, free of implication or the devious music of strategy. For Jesse, it mixed with his mother's laugh, and tumbled down into his most secret spot, presenting him with what he regarded as happiness.

"You're luminous," he suddenly said to Lois, stopping all of them in their tracks, as if they had spotted a deer in the woods.

Their silence caused Amy to look up from the corn, and the two clerks to glance across the room.

"That's very pleasing to hear," Lois said at last.

"I meant it factually," Jesse said, putting his arm around

his father's waist, thinking, I'm closer to this guy than I know.

"Please come for lunch," Lois said.

"Lunch," Jesse said. "A *Lois* lunch."

"Ah," Lois said.

"No imposition?" Norman said.

"Please don't insult me," Lois said with a smile.

"Amy," Jesse called out as she crossed the floor to join them, "this is a friend of my mother's, of ours. Her name is Lois Hayes."

LOIS AND DAN Allenson's beach house was on the ocean and filled with light. There were no shades or curtains, just bulky comfortable chairs and couches, and lithographs of Cape Cod—misty summer afternoons, muted morning light, dunes stretching beyond the frames in their pale gray. In the living room above the fireplace hung a remarkable and intense painting of an enormous pumpkin that thrilled Jesse with its clarity, its meticulous detail. Just a pumpkin by a window, with pumpkin light passing through open shutters.

"That has eyes," Lois said to Jesse when she saw his interest.

"I'll say," he replied, standing up close to it, letting his fingertips touch it gently. "It's so strong."

"Now *that* is something your mother would have cherished," Lois said.

"No doubt." Norman carefully let himself fall into a pillowy rocking chair.

Lois opened a bottle of white wine and brought glasses.

The kitchen was part of the living room; from its large oak dining table there was a full view of Norman's rocking chair.

14

Lois began to pull lunch together as they talked. She glided around her kitchen as if she were standing on some smooth-running apparatus, a collection of wheels that made no sound, that glided her into the corners and cabinets with which she was so familiar. Jesse imagined a choreography, Lois on a stage, moving to charming music.

Lois appeared to him precisely as he recalled her from seventeen years earlier. Her smoky voice settled him in as it always had, foot-rubbing, soothing. Wound-healing.

And there now! Flashes of green and yellow: a salad. And weakfish, cleaned and ready on a cutting board. Four portions of fish, as if guests had been expected. And corn from the Green Thumb that Lois had just bought. And the purposeful wine, lotionary and encouraging.

"Dan's in the city," Lois said, with her back momentarily to the group. "He'll be sorry he missed you."

"Lawyers," Norman said. "You never were much interested in musicians. Lawyers are always suing musicians for one thing or another."

"Your memory fails," Lois said to Norman, turning around to offer an unnegotiable smile.

"Not really," Norman said, puzzling Jesse. What was this secret language?

"This is such a pretty house," Amy said, sipping her wine. She was centrally seated almost directly in front of the stunning pumpkin. Jesse found that her lavish red hair conflicted with the painting.

"Do you remember the time I took you and Carol to a dress rehearsal of a George Kaufman play?" Norman asked Lois.

"I think so," Lois said, "but go on."

"If you'll remember, we were all standing in the back with George, watching a simply dreadful performance. At the

15

intermission George disappeared. When he came back, you'll remember that he told us that he'd sent a telegram to the cast. I think it was you, Lois, who asked him what the telegram had said. It said: 'AM IN THE BACK OF THE THEATER. WISH YOU WERE HERE.'"

Lois remembered. "It was Carol who asked," she said, which Jesse weighed as possibly true.

"Did I ever tell you, Jesse, about visiting Jed Harris, the producer, with Kaufman?" Norman was leaning forward as best he could in a rocking chair.

"Tell Lois and Amy," Jesse said, annoyed at-"the producer." Norman constantly identified the recognizable: Leonard Bernstein, the conductor; Irwin Shaw, the writer; Walter Kerr, the critic.

"And this is absolutely true," Norman said, as he frequently did.

"George and I went over to Jed Harris's apartment on some business—I forget what. When we arrived, Jed opened the door. In the nude. We said nothing. We came in and sat down, and the three of us must have talked a couple of hours."

"This guy was naked all that time?" Amy said.

"Throughout the entire meeting," Norman said. "Jed Harris remained totally and completely naked."

"So what happened?" Amy asked, holding her glass of wine in her lap.

"So what happened?" Norman said, glancing at Amy, but speaking to Lois. "I'll tell you what happened. When we finally got up to leave, Jed walked us to the door. Keep in mind that we had never acknowledged his condition. As we left, George said to Harris: 'Jed, your fly's open.'"

"Yes," Lois said with a laugh, appearing to remember.

"Those were the days of Max Gordon, the producer," Norman went on. "And this will interest you, Amy."

Jesse saw that his father was confined to his stories, his real truth trapped in despair, hidden away like Otto Frank's family, prohibited from moving around during the day. Only at night, Jesse imagined, did his father permit himself the painful luxury of anguish. Alone in his office, the curtains securely drawn, he could thrash it out in solitary. Deprived of an audience for his set pieces, he was left with his own regrets. In broad daylight Norman lay in camouflage telling his tales.

"Max Gordon was a famous producer in the theater long before you were born," Norman was telling Amy. "One day, before an opening of a Max Gordon show, the *New York Times* came to interview him for a Sunday piece. The reporter asked Max some questions unrelated to the theater, one of which was: 'Mr. Gordon, do you believe in reincarnation?' Max replied: 'Of course I do. I can't believe we close here and don't open somewhere else.' "

Norman had been right about Amy. She loved the story, this girlfriend of his who believed—in fact, *knew*—that once upon a time, many years ago, many years before Max Gordon, she herself had been a grasshopper. She had told this to Jesse on the way into New York from Larchmont, Dom Perignon helping her along. Jesse, uncontentious and mellow, had replied, "It wouldn't surprise me."

"A Lois lunch," Jesse said when they were all seated around the oak table.

Lois had put on an album of Norman's music to accompany the weakfish.

"I *remember* this," Norman said. "There's some nice writing for strings on this album."

"You wrote all these songs?" Amy said, holding an ear of corn in both hands.

"He did," Jesse said. "I've played you this record."

"I guess I didn't realize the extent of it," Amy said.

"I've thought of you whenever I've heard one of your songs," Lois said. "I know every one of them."

"Not the new things for *Roman Holiday*," Norman said.

"You mean a musical based on the movie?"

"If we ever get a book," Norman said.

"Who's going to play Rome?" Lois asked.

"Count on Lois to go to the heart of the matter," Norman said, smiling. "From anyone else, that could be taken as a belligerent remark."

"Why?" Lois asked.

Then Jesse remembered. Lois was funny. Lois was wonderfully cruel, but who would care? She was so artful, no one ever minded. That was what was soothing about her. Even with her arrows at the ready, she granted diplomatic immunity to the closest people in her life. She wouldn't harm you for the world, though beneath her guilelessness buzzed a cartoon villain with a bagful of tricks. *Who's going to play Rome.* Rome, the real star of the movie. Jesse thought that Norman might as well throw in the towel this very day. No libretto out of the San Fernando Valley would run a month at the Mark Hellinger with Oliver Smith's Rome dangling cheaply behind Norman's earnest music.

"Ray Bolger can play Rome," Jesse said. "Trust me on this one."

Norman ate a full meal, and seconds. His eyes shone with trust, despite Rome, Ray Bolger, and any other potshots he might imagine lay in store. To Jesse, he looked like Carol's husband and his own youthful father, sitting with his wife on a park bench, Jesse tangled up in their love, playing at their feet, leaping on their laps, arms everywhere, hugging, holding.

After lunch they sat on the deck overlooking the ocean.

The tide was out and the water was calm. Sea gulls swooped over their heads and gathered at water's edge.

"What a lovely day," Amy said, her chin resting on her knees.

"It would have been nice to meet Dan," Norman said. "Perhaps in the city."

"Yes," Lois said.

"You and lawyers," Norman said. "Did I ever tell you what Alan Lerner told me just before he got married for the sixth time?"

The question was for Jesse, the answer was yes, though Jesse replied no.

"Alan said that you never really knew a woman until you met her across the floor of a courtroom."

"Dan never dealt with Alan Jay Lerner," Lois said. "He's a First Amendment kind of guy."

"How long have you been married?" Jesse asked Lois.

"Three years," she answered, "come New Year's Eve."

Jesse figured it out: for thirteen years she had wandered around, unencumbered by children, the world filled with friends and postcards. There must have been some money in her jeans, and cunning suitors gregariously presenting themselves in diversified ports of call. In 1966 a First Amendment guy had whispered to her with fashionable reason. Lois, a honey of a catch, accustomed to being alone, relinquished her first marriage at long last, and settled on a New Year's Eve as a second starting point. If she was exactly Carol's age, she'd be fifty-five. And now here—Lois Hayes Allenson on a deck above the ocean, years and years after closing her door to Norman and Jesse Savitt with a glossy photo of one of the world's tallest buildings. Goodbye.

"This is very much like the day Leland Hayward phoned

Irving Berlin from Malibu," Jesse heard his father say in the distance.

———————

"WELL," LOIS SAID, easing them out to the car. "It's been quite a lucky day."

To Jesse's surprise, she took Norman's hand as they walked down the driveway.

Jesse put his arm around Amy, touching her for the first time that day.

"The pumpkin is yours, you know," Lois said to Jesse by the car door.

"What do you mean?" he asked, not understanding.

"I want you to have that painting. I'll have it crated and sent."

"Don't be absurd," Jesse said, protesting honestly.

"I'll take no argument on this," Lois said. "Your father has given me the address."

"When did he give you the address?" Jesse asked.

"Along the way," Lois said.

"Please," Jesse said, beginning to hush up.

"Enough," Lois said.

"Why?" Jesse asked.

"I have my reasons," Lois said.

Norman embraced Lois and kissed her good-bye on the cheek. Jesse followed with a tender hug.

"You're settled," Norman said to Lois as he got into the car.

"It's visible, isn't it," Lois replied.

Jesse drove them slowly away from the house, and waved a last good-bye to Lois, who still stood where the car had been.

"That beautiful painting," Amy said.

"The Empire State disguised as a pumpkin," Jesse said.

They drove in silence through Bridgehampton and Watermill, and passed the Green Thumb, which was closed for the day. The sun was lost to clouds. Jesse felt it possible that it would rain on the way home.

"Did I ever tell you about Harry Barrett?" Norman said, breaking the long quiet.

"What about Harry Barrett," Jesse said, looking over to Amy, whose eyes were closed.

"This is an absolutely true story. I don't know why it comes to mind."

"What about Harry Barrett," Jesse repeated.

"Harry Barrett was an old-time songwriter. He had some pop hits, made a little money. When he was a young boy—I think he was about six or seven years old—his father deserted the family. They had been living in the Chicago area, and his father just left them and disappeared. And the family never saw him again.

"One day, a few years ago, Harry Barrett was in the process of making a tour of radio stations around the country to promote his catalog, and he found himself sitting in the lobby of a St. Louis hotel, waiting for a publicist to pick him up and take him to several interviews.

"As he sat there he saw a man sitting across the lobby whom he recognized immediately as his father. There was just no question about it.

"So, Harry Barrett went over to the guy, looked down at him, and said, 'Hello Dad.' "

"It really *was* his father?" Jesse said, never having heard this one before.

"It was," Norman said.

"What happened?"

"They talked for a while, very generally. The father, it seems, was a traveling salesman working St. Louis. He asked Harry what business *he* was in. Harry told him that he was a songwriter. They chatted a little while longer, until the publicist arrived to take Harry Barrett to his appointments.

"Harry said to his father, 'It was nice to see you.' And do you know what his father said? Do you know what he said as they parted? He said to Harry Barrett, 'It was nice to see you, too. You know something? I'd never met a songwriter before.'"

OVER THE PURPLE HILLS

Norman Savitt drove up to visit his son in the school's dormitory. It was a difficult trip from the city to the small west Connecticut town where Norman had found a place for his ten-year-old: a dorm with private rooms and clean hallways, a school with a bit of a reputation. Jesse had told his father that he understood why he had to live at school—that his mother was sick, that his mother was in bed all the time, that his dad was in California a lot of the time, that it was "the very best thing to do."

"The *only* thing, for now," Norman had said. "For now," Norman had repeated.

He was making his second trip since the beginning of school. This time, Sunday morning of Thanksgiving weekend, the going was tough. A light snow was falling, windblown and tricky in the gray November light. Norman had an early Christmas gift for Jesse, a baseball glove from FAO Schwarz. Jesse had told him on the phone that all he wanted to do for the rest of his life was to have a catch with someone, "all day every day right through the winter and spring and next summer and all next year."

At the school's gate Norman had to get out of the car and use the phone on the brick wall to reach the front office and announce his arrival.

It was one o'clock as Norman inched along the pebbled driveway for the three-quarters of a mile to the parking area near the dorm. How distant this was from seven that morning when he had put Carol on a train to North Carolina, where she would join an experimental diet program for hypertension.

Norman was forty-eight, with both members of his immediate family under guard, miles from home, miles from the hotel in which they lived. He was visiting one of them today, and the other next week in Durham. He imagined sadly that he would visit them forever, that it would go on and on, like Jesse's idea of a catch. He got out of the car and walked through the snow without realizing that he was wearing Jesse's glove.

The dorm, with its long dimly lit halls and cubbyhole rooms and clamoring radiators, served as a headquarters for the disengaged, boys who were far too young for vigorous schoolwork, boys from Latin America and Japan and Germany and Texas, who showered centrally under fluorescent lights and brushed their teeth with Calox powder, and, barefoot on the cold stone floor, returned to their rooms for lights out at nine.

Norman knew what Jesse believed; his son had leaked it all out in bits and pieces. Jesse believed that his parents were right. He was different from all the other boys he knew, and deserved to be in a dormitory with foreign exchange students because he himself was a foreigner. He didn't know how to behave. He was so unusually improper that both his mother and father, as loving as they were, as famous as they were, with famous friends to whose houses they would go, in whose houses special meals would be prepared for Jesse's mother because of her illness—that's how *loved* his parents were—couldn't have a life worth living if Jesse was actually around. And, besides, they lived in a hotel with just one bedroom and a living room and a kitchen and a hallway to the back door where they threw out the garbage, and there wasn't any room for him, even if he were a perfect boy, a perfect son. So they did what they had to do, which was to find a dormitory *and* a school in the very same place, so that he could have everything all at once and not be a bother in a hotel.

Jo Stafford was singing behind Jesse's closed door. Before knocking, Norman listened for a moment: " 'In the night, though we're apart, there's a ghost of you within my haunted heart.' "

"Daddy!" Jesse said, with a hug and face kisses and another big hug.

Jesse's window overlooked the woods in which the school was set. His mother had sent up a bright orange rug, a porcelain desk lamp, a lithograph of a sailboat on a winter lake, a thick brown quilt, a small record player, and blue curtains with teddy bears and flowers that Jesse had stored under the bed. He had thumbtacked baseball cards to a bulletin board of his own, and to a calendar with Disney characters in the corners. He had put a line through each passing day. Norman, sitting on the bed, noticed that April 14 of the next year, 1949, was circled. He asked about it.

"Baseball begins," Jesse said.

"Is this the right glove?" Norman asked.

"It's *absolutely* great. It's just like my old glove."

Norman knew where Jesse had picked up "absolutely." He heard himself along the way: "The show was *absolutely* great." "I've written an *absolutely* great song." He saw himself

27

as exaggerated and false, the pretensions of the theater seeping out, and into his son.

Jesse had stacks of records on the floor: Norman's own songs, Kern, Rachmaninoff, Rodgers. Jesse wanted his father to hear some of them. He played Nat Cole, Frankie Laine, Peggy Lee.

Norman had brought a picnic lunch he had left in the car.

"Could we have a catch?" Jesse asked excitedly.

"It's snowing," Norman said.

"Just on the way to the car?"

"But it's *really* snowing," Norman said.

"It doesn't matter, there's no one on the field."

"I don't have a glove," Norman said.

"I have two, the old one and the new one."

"But I need a lefty glove."

"Raphael has one," Jesse said. "Please, Daddy."

Raphael, an eleven-year-old Cuban, didn't reply to Jesse's knock. Jesse opened his door.

The room was a warehouse of comic books and Mr. Goodbars. Small crucifixes were nailed to all four walls. A pile of clothes lay in the middle of the floor; Jesse found the baseball glove beneath them.

The wind had subsided a bit, but the snow had not. They made their way slowly through it to the deserted playing field.

"Get out there!" Jesse shouted to his father.

Norman felt the sting of Jesse's throw through Raphael's flimsy mitt. At first his returns were wild, making Jesse run. Jesse dug the ball out of the snow time and again, until his father became more accurate.

"You're *great* at this!" Jesse shouted, after a time.

Norman was exhilarated. "Make me run for one!" he shouted.

Jesse tossed one high.

Norman, on the run, even through the snow, even in his long overcoat, caught up with it.

"Great!" Jesse yelled. "Absolutely great!"

"One more!" Norman shouted into a gust of wind and blowing snow.

Jesse threw another that was harder to play.

Norman reached it at the last moment.

"Norman DiMaggio!" Jesse yelled, his voice cracking up there so high.

"COULD WE EAT in the car?" Jesse asked, on the way to the parking area.

"It's too cold," Norman said.

"We could leave the engine running so it'll be warm," Jesse said.

"You really want to?" Norman said, giving in.

"We'll just sit in the back like passengers."

"We're bundled up."

"It'll make me feel like we're going on a trip together. It's like somebody's driving us."

"Where?" Norman asked as they reached the car.

"I don't know. Maybe home, for a visit or something. I mean, I wouldn't *stay,* or anything."

Norman had roast beef sandwiches, Cokes and Oreos.

They sat in the back of the car in their overcoats, dropping crumbs into the cloth napkins that Carol had insisted Norman take. "Do you have the napkins?" she had asked, standing by the train that morning.

While Jesse talked about baseball, Norman imagined his drive back home, back to the Volney Hotel, up the elevator to the sixteenth floor, the suite immaculate, vacuumed and dusted by the noontime maids.

He would arrive to face Carol's absence. He would call her in Durham. He saw himself sitting on her side of the bed, his elbows resting on his knees, Carol being called to what Norman imagined as a phone booth in a hall, a long-distance hiss making it difficult to hear. How was the trip? he would ask. What kind of room do you have. When do you see Dr. Klempner. What is a good time to call. It's snowing here. Is it snowing there. I love you. Do you love me?

"Did Mommy leave this morning?" Jesse asked, shifting out of baseball.

Norman hoped that Jesse hadn't noticed that his father had been miles away.

"Early this morning," Norman said, sipping a Coke. "Everything was right on time, everything was just fine. The regimen down there will help her. People from all over the world go down there."

"Will it cure her?" Jesse asked.

"We just don't know," Norman said.

Jesse had never been told how seriously ill his mother was, how frightened his father was of any ringing telephone. "Mr. Savitt, it's for you." And the news, handed out by a stranger, or a doctor, or a concierge with an accent. "Mr. Savitt, the woman you married on July twelfth, 1934, the mother of your son, Jesse, has died."

"What's the worst that can happen?" Jesse asked.

"Your mother is the strongest woman I know," Norman said.

When they were finished eating, they got out of the car to face another gust of wind that blew the snow around, forcing them to hurry back to the dorm. Inside, they took seats across from each other in the leisure room, while Raphael lay on his stomach reading comic books.

Norman told Jesse about the show he was writing. Jesse already knew some of his father's new melodies. He had memorized them on first hearing, and many times after lights out he had sung them quietly to himself.

"What's the road schedule?" Jesse asked.

"New Haven, April first. Then the Wilbur in Boston, April nineteenth. Then the Majestic, May something, probably the ninth. And I've got an absolutely *great* Western kind of song. Is there a piano here?" Norman asked.

There was an upright on the stage in the gym. "The doors might be locked because of the holidays," Jesse said.

"Let's try," Norman said. "Raphael, do you want to come?"

"Where," Raphael said.

"No he doesn't," Jesse said impatiently. "Let's do it alone. *Please.*"

"Certainly," Norman said, recognizing his error.

"Stay here," Jesse said to Raphael.

"Where," Raphael said.

Jesse led his father across the playing field, their old footprints vanished in the fresh white snow.

They entered the school's main building through the kitchen, and walked in single file down a dark corridor to an indoor playroom, through two locker rooms and up a flight of stairs.

The gym was open, the largest room in the school, used for chapel in the morning, and basketball, and for theatrical productions on a stage at the far end.

A hundred metal chairs faced the stage, left in place through the holidays after the Thanksgiving service Wednesday afternoon.

Jesse took a seat in the fourth row.

"You're my *best* audience," Norman shouted, going to the stage, his voice ringing out in the strange, unaccommodating acoustics of the gymnasium.

"This is a *Western* song," Norman told Jesse again. "A sort of cowboy song. I think it's absolutely one of the *best* melodies I've ever written."

"Does it have a title?" Jesse asked.

"It's called 'Over the Purple Hills.' Isn't that a nice title? The lyric, when I write it, will say something like, over the purple hills on the other side of somewhere, there's magic and peace. And only people with determination can get there. Do you know what *serene* means? It means a lack of trouble in your heart. Well, *that's* over the purple hills. Do you understand?"

"Sure," Jesse said, from the fourth row. "Is everything purple there?"

"No. It's very light. It's filled with sun. Like the day on Long Island when you said you could see France. That kind of real sun and clarity. The purple is deep in the mountains."

"I see," Jesse said.

"I have only one line of the lyric, and then I'll just play the rest of the melody."

Norman sat formally at the piano for a moment or two, gathering in Jesse's complete attention.

" 'Over the purple hills, far away, far far away,' " he sang in his clear, familiar baritone, the piano woefully out of tune.

Blowing snow swirled outside the windows. The gym, unlit, was bathed in white. Jesse felt himself rising into the air, still seated on his metal chair. His father's melody held him high above everyone.

THE
LAST
AND
ONLY
MESSENGER

Julia left a message on Jesse's answering machine. Since their divorce she had mastered neutrality, banishing the parody through which they had communicated from the start. They had courted largely through laughter; they poked lovingly at the vulnerable spots in each other. Their wedding day, six years earlier in 1979, celebrated the pleasure of their satire. They were a sophisticated comic item, Julia and Jesse. So much so that even now, with both remarried, Jesse wished to keep it going. He wanted their friendship. But Julia, with more wisdom than he, kept her distance, leaning just a little to the side of irritation. Jesse offered no resistance, allowing her the daily choices. Today on his machine she offered nothing at all but the facts: she and Annie, their two-year-old daughter, were going to "take a little picnic by the carousel in the park at twelve-thirty," if he wanted to join them. It was all for Annie, the voice implied. If you think I want you at our picnic you're nuts, but a girl needs her father, so that's where we'll be. And yet, Jesse knew, some part of Julia's heart would welcome him. If all else failed, the sympathy vote would do it: Norman's stroke,

Jesse's daily visits to New York Hospital, Norman's garbled talk, his irreversible paralysis, his tears.

Before lunch in the park, Jesse went to visit his father. He read theater grosses from *Variety* to Norman, and the *Times* review of a new musical.

Norman paid attention for a little while before slipping into despair. Jesse was trying to talk about Annie when he saw Norman's mind drift away. "She can say 'avocado,' " he was telling his father, but felt that from within the jumble of language left by the stroke, Norman wanted to communicate regret. "Slower, talk slower," Jesse said. "I didn't get it, try again."

It occurred to him that his father and daughter were each grappling with words, equal partners in mumbo jumbo, while Julia floated in her lake of "obfuscate" and "pernicious" and lilted along to impressive climaxes that absorbed any gesture of retort.

———

ON HIS BIKE, heading to the park from the hospital, Jesse thought of his father's regret. Was there an apology in there somewhere? And why now, with their slates wiped mostly clean, issues resolved? He was lucky that they had dealt with the dirt, that they had forgiven each other. This old man was going on eighty-five—a good span across the twentieth century.

Norman regretted failure, no doubt. These failures had surely come to haunt him in that hospital room, as he lay there with no itinerary, tied to an IV. Norman was trying to tell Jesse all about it, but couldn't work his way to it. That crucial part of his brain had been struck by lightning, and he was reduced to animal sounds. Jesse heard those same sounds from other rooms along the hall in Neurology, a special language—minimalism, Jesse thought, but with an occasional burst of clarity, like Annie handing out "avocado" in the midst of babble.

And Molly, now his wife after years of knowing her, caught with Jesse in a torrent of lucid pleading: Listen to me! She lay in wait with a fresh approach to a resolved issue. And Jesse, on his toes, quick and facile, until they were both knotted in italics, exhausted, falling to the bed, where for years they had conducted their most successful business.

Jesse pulled his bike up by their bench near the carousel, which pumped forth its calliope music—"And the Band Played On."

Jesse picked out a piece of the lyric as a greeting. " 'His brain it was loaded, it nearly exploded, the poor girl she quaked with alarm,' " he said cheerfully, addressing Annie but speaking to Julia.

"Yum," Annie said, holding out a peanut butter and jelly sandwich to her father.

"May I have a bite?" he said, bending down.

"You can have a whole one of your own," Julia said. "You shouldn't take bites of people's food anymore," she went on. "It's not becoming."

"Becoming," Jesse said. "What an understandable word from a girl like you."

"Take your own sandwich," she said, pulling it out from her bag and handing it to him.

He sat down next to Annie and offered her a bite.

"Is Daddy's same as me?" Annie asked Julia.

"Yes," Jesse told Annie. "But mine's just a little better."

Annie reached for his sandwich and took a bite.

"Can we change?" she asked him.

"Sure, if it's OK with Mommy."

Julia didn't offer an opinion, her professional indifference allowing the deal.

The three of them sat without talking, Julia and Jesse watching Annie drip jelly to the ground.

Jesse recalled last night's dream, his first school dream in many years: trapped in a bed, in a dormitory in an unfamiliar city, lying there, grown up, thinking of Molly. A committee of three arrived to evaluate his performance. Total strangers. His room was untidy. A television set was on, transmitting trash.

He was asked his age.

"Forty-six," he replied, contemptuously.

He had attended no classes, engaged in no debates, created no friendships, displayed no interests. An empty bottle of Scotch rolled out from under his bed.

"Molly won't wait forever," Jesse said.

———————

"SO WHAT'S THE schedule," Julia said.

Jesse considered answering: I've created no friendships.

Forty-six, with everyone around him twenty-five years younger. He had been away from the academy a sufficient number of weeks and months to marry twice, become a father, earn a wage, conduct affairs with women, assault two men with his own hands, pass judgment on the integrity of others, attend to his father in a hospital.

"I had a dream about school last night," he said.

"So what's the schedule," Julia said.

Jesse had hoped that after her own recent remarriage Julia would relax a bit, play a little, like old times. But for the moment, even with calliope music and dripping jelly and a beautiful spring day, she wouldn't come around.

"The schedule is, tomorrow I have Annie until four. Isn't that the schedule?"

Jesse wished he could go further, wished he could dance with Julia, with this savvy and heroic ex-wife of his. She loved Artie Shaw and all the old music. He would buy her compact discs of everything, of Caruso, of Sinatra singing "You'll Never Know." But she would think such gifts were inappropriate and confusing: What are you tellin' me, big boy, are you comin' or goin' or what?

"Balloon!" Annie shouted with a full mouth.

"I'll get you one," Jesse said. "What color?"

"Red," Annie said, pointing.

Returning to them with a red balloon, Jesse was swept by his love for Annie; her almond eyes and dark skin, her simply wonderful face housing both of her parents. Jesse knew that he would gladly die for this child, that there would be not a moment of hesitation. He would lie down on the tracks and await the train with equanimity.

"Balloon!" Annie shouted, taking the string.

"How's Norman," Julia asked.

"Not progressing," Jesse said.

"I wanna sit here," Annie said, standing, the balloon in one hand, the sandwich in the other.

She arranged the three of them with herself in the middle.

She tucked her right leg under her. With her sandwich hand she pointed up. "Is there a ceiling in the sky?" she asked her parents, her head back, her happy eyes searching the blue.

IN THE MIDDLE of the night Jesse woke up, inflicted with his father. Molly lay asleep on her back. "Your nose grows much larger at night," he had told her once.

"It's the lies in my dreams," she had replied.

He went into the living room and sat on the sofa without turning the light on.

Why so much dreaming?

His father, springtime, the tangle of women and children.

"Don't tell anything," Norman had managed that afternoon, in one split second of clarity.

Jesse had understood. Only Jesse. The others had fallen by the wayside, into graves circled by the tearful. Or they were in California, or in England, or in Brooklyn, vanished, those who would know, those who'd had an inkling.

Jesse saw himself as the only messenger left, running through the night, bearing information of interest to new generations, to Annie, and, as Norman would have it, way beyond, into the accusing future.

Norman's secrets had gathered power as he lay for weeks in the hospital, through those nights, through those sponge baths, the suspended television set delivering the same trash as in Jesse's dream.

Annie would rely on Jesse's information. She would turn to the last and only messenger for the facts. What would he say? Your sensational grandfather spent the last twenty years of his life imagining himself a failure, picking through the debris of financial misadventures, observing a weakening social grasp, and experiencing an ongoing despair peculiar for its severity in such a vivid spirit. What your grandfather saw in the mirror was a bum at the ball.

Jesse turned on the small lamp by the sofa. On the coffee table in front of him, framed in silver, was a photograph of Norman holding Annie. Annie, five days old, home from the hospital, wrapped in a white blanket. Norman was holding her stiffly, holding her not at all, really; she lay on his wrists, an exhibition on loan.

"They passed in the night," Molly said the first time she saw this one picture of Norman and Annie together. A recent gift from Julia.

Norman died in the hospital on the first of June. Jesse was called; it was nearly dawn. He and Molly went to the hospital.

They saw to the cremation, spent nearly a week going through Norman's things. All those letters and papers. Photos of Norman out in the world: black-and-white-checkered shoes in California during the war; a tailored winter suit at Seventy-second and Fifth; with Jesse's mother on a sun deck in Bridgehampton, Norman held a drink, Jesse's mother a folded rotogravure, she resembled Annie.

And there was Norman thirteen years earlier in a house on Cape Cod during a thunderstorm. Jesse himself had taken the picture.

They had waited out the rain together. They had talked about Molly for a while. The sky was dark. Black. They could barely see the ocean, though they were on top of it.

"I suggest you marry her," Norman said.

Jesse married Julia first.

MAX

He was fifty-five; Jesse Savitt was sixteen and "wild."

"He's a wild kid. He's very bright, but he doesn't apply himself, and he runs around this school without regard for anyone else."

"Norman, there's a wild streak in that son of yours. You're in no way to blame, believe me."

"Mr. Savitt, we think private tutoring is necessary in this case as an adjunct to his studies, to encourage a broader perspective and a thought-provoking interplay, a one-on-one, if you will, that might subdue a tendency to a kind of wild and undisciplined performance that we've observed at this school."

Max Bookstein sat in Norman Savitt's living room, smoking Camel cigarettes, learning about Jesse, the boy he would tutor. Norman Savitt offered good money, and Max was broke and in debt, a math professor at Hofstra, a midnight novelist, an insomniac, the father of one Michael Bookstein of Boston University—a freshman, Class of 1958.

Max was divorced. Helen, his former wife, was still single eight years later; Max sent her five hundred dollars a month.

They had last spoken lengthily on Christmas Day of 1948. "Let's touch base now and again," Helen had said at Longchamp's, at lunch. They never touched base again, not about Michael Bookstein, not about Adlai Stevenson. Only Helen's scribbled endorsements on the back of Max's checks passed as correspondence. After two years Max had stopped turning the checks over to look at Helen's signature, had given up (as he put it to himself) reading his mail.

Norman Savitt, a widower with one child, had been told about Max Bookstein by a teacher at Jesse's school. To him, Bookstein looked disheveled and intense; he sat forward on the couch, chain-smoking, using his hands to emphasize his points. His tie was askew, his brown suit rumpled, and, most disquietingly, his teeth were a light brown—cigarettes, no doubt, but possibly, Norman thought, due in part to a flow of venom. Bookstein was a live wire, probably with a network of complicated arrangements that more often than not worked against him, riling him, forcing him to speak badly of many people, abusively, cigarette ashes falling everywhere as he accused. And yet, listen to him here—possibly a pose to get the job, but still—listen to him: "The key to mathematics—*any* kind, in Jesse's case, geometry—is literature. Words. Tolstoy, Chekhov, Dickens, your basic mathematicians. It's the *overview* that matters. Numbers are letters shaped differently. One must learn how to read before tackling questions. Does your son really know how to read?"

"Yes," Norman replied.

"Well, that's fine," Max said, his face relaxing into a smile. "I think we'll be able to work together fluently."

Norman hired Max partly because of the word "fluently," and partly because his son had always sat on the edge of his own seat, leaning forward all the while, italics flowing, excitement everywhere, even when its cause was less than apparent to Norman. Oh, yes, a sporting event, Norman could understand that, but asparagus, a modest snowfall, didn't, *shouldn't* attract as enthusiastic an audience as Jesse generally became. Rather than hire a docile sort, why not Max Bookstein, one of Jesse's own. The cigarettes: so what. The brown teeth: what's the difference.

Jesse came home from school as Max was leaving.

"This is the gentleman," Norman said to Jesse.

"Did you see the Parliaments?" Jesse asked Max.

Jesse took Max into his father's study. From the ceiling, well over fifty cigarettes hung like birthday candles upside down, mysteriously held in place.

"You're asking yourself how," Jesse said. "You're asking yourself why. You're asking yourself: Should I take this job."

Jesse took a pack of Parliaments from his father's desk.

"Look see," he said to Max. "If you bend the tip of the filter, like so, and then apply just a little moisture with your tongue, like so, this will cause a suction phenomenon. Now look. You've got to throw the cigarette straight up. The ceiling has to be low, of course. The Sistine Chapel is out, though it would certainly make for an amusing project. Like *so.* You just throw it like that."

The cigarette stuck to the ceiling, joining the many others. "You try it," Jesse said.

Max tried and tried. Norman watched from the doorway. Max wouldn't give up, his own lighted Camel dangling from his lips.

Finally he succeeded. "My God!" he said triumphantly, incredulously.

"Arthur Garfield Hayes was here a month ago, right, Daddy? He couldn't do it, he was too old. He couldn't get the cigarette up to the ceiling. It was chilling."

NORMAN BOUGHT a card table at which his son and Max could work. Jesse's room, small and tidy, was lined with shelves of books and records that spilled over into neat piles on the floor that had to be moved into the corners of the room to allow for the new working surface.

"Why so dark?" Max asked.

"I can see better," Jesse said.

Max came three times a week at eight in the evening. They sat at the card table by a floor lamp borrowed from the living room, Jesse's geometry books spread out before them. Late in their first session they let geometry fall away.

"Do you follow baseball?" Jesse asked.

"Casually," Max said. "I'm aware of the story."

"What do you mean by 'story'?"

"It's a story, don't you see? It's every day, with many layers of meaning, and at the end the characters have experienced a change. They're not the same people they were at the beginning. Year by year the stories accumulate. They're interrelated, even though generations go by, so that the stories, when they're put together, constitute a collection. While I couldn't be considered a baseball expert, I have an understanding of how the book was written, and by whom. I'm a part of the readership."

Jesse had many questions for Max. Max lived on Seventy-eighth Street and Second Avenue. Max was divorced. Max had a son in college whom he hadn't seen in a long time. Max was writing a novel that he didn't especially want to talk about; he had about six hundred double-spaced pages, and that was *it* on *that* subject. Max owned a 1953 Mercury, which he drove to Hofstra. Max had a three-room apartment. Max was fifty-five, with a birthday coming up on January 2. And Max answered honestly when Jesse asked, at the start of their third session, "No, Jesse, I don't have a girlfriend at the moment."

"Is he worth the money?" Norman asked Jesse.

They were walking through the zoo together on a Saturday afternoon, and had stopped to watch the seals being fed.

"He's wonderful, if that's what you mean," Jesse said.

"Do you get any work done? You always seem to be talking about something else when you come out of there."

"Of course we do," Jesse said. "Do you know that he has seven thousand books? Wow. Isn't that something? That's more books than anybody, I'll bet you."

"He's regarded highly at Hofstra, I know that," Norman said, having checked it all out. Bookstein, rumpled though he was, had developed a following on campus.

"His classes are most desired," Norman had been told.

And Bookstein was punctual, eight on the button, even on the night of the November hurricane. What a sight he'd been that night, with no raincoat or hat, just his brown suit sopping wet, his thinning hair matted to his head, the knot of his wide yellow tie halfway up the right side of his neck, clump, his black cordovans filled with water. Clump, down the hall to Jesse's room, oblivious of his footprints on the light green carpet as he lit a Camel.

"Is he helping you to understand?" Norman asked. "That's what you always said, that you didn't understand anything to do with numbers."

"What I understand is, numbers are important to get you through school. You've got to know them and memorize combinations of them and hang on to them for dear life until you pass the subject. I've learned that I've got to do that. What makes a teacher a *math* teacher is that they keep thinking about them—the numbers—after it's permissible to forget them. I think Max is very unusual because he's very sophisticated and really well read and everything, and he's a writer. Daddy, he's got a thousand pages of a book, maybe more, but he's really cool about it. He's modest about it. So, you see, he's unusual because he's got a choice. I mean, he understands how everything works. He doesn't have to *retain* the numbers if he doesn't want to."

"He'd better retain them, he teaches them," Norman said.

"That's because he *enjoys* them, in *spite* of them."

MAX GOT THE flu in February and canceled his sessions for the week.

"It's those cigarettes," Norman said. "It weakens his resistance."

And the candy, Jesse thought. All those Goobers chocolate-coated peanuts, just like the ones at the RKO 86th Street Theater—only, they were his dinner.

"I don't need to eat much or sleep much, it seems," Max had said.

"Do you have breakfast?" Jesse had asked.

"Only coffee. I'm not hungry then."

"When are you hungry?"

"I'm too busy. That's the honest truth," Max had said.

Jesse looked up Max's number in the phone book.

"Can I come and see you?" he asked.

"I don't want to infect you," Max said, coughing badly, more severely than usual, more gratingly than his usual "Camel call."

"You won't infect me," Jesse said. "I promise."

"No, really I don't think so," Max said. "I think it would be a bad idea."

Jesse went anyway. From a courtyard below Max's third-floor window he yelled up, after his buzzing received no response. He knew it was Max's window; he could see book-shelves to the ceiling, and the special kind of light created by cigarette smoke.

Max, in pajamas, opened the window. "I told you no," he said, gently enough for Jesse to understand that he would gain entry. Besides, it was sleeting. Jesse could see himself down there in the courtyard, shivering, concerned for his best friend, the best friend maybe missing Jesse, wanting to talk, and there Jesse was, having come all the way across town from Central Park West, bearing Goobers chocolate-coated peanuts in the event Max Bookstein proved stub-born.

"Well, come on up, but be careful of the stairs, some of them are tricky."

Tricky meant wobbly, with weak banisters, and ants, and obscenities in crayon on the walls, all the way up to apart-ment 3A, where Max welcomed Jesse at the door. He had put on a bathrobe, and stood barefoot and wheezing, hold-ing a lit cigarette. Jesse realized that Max wore a mustache, had always worn a mustache, not just a little cartoon line of a thing but a bushy growth, lively and obvious. Jesse had never noticed it, or at most, had never considered it.

"Come in, come in, come in," Max said, with an only slightly threatening impatience.

The apartment was as Max had described it: books every-where, in the thousands, there was no doubt. The rooms were quite small, the whole apartment oppressively hot. The furniture, what little Max had—a double bed, one couch, two stiff-backed wooden chairs, a desk covered with typewritten pages, a footstool in the kitchenette—was threadbare, chipped, unsightly. The radiators rattled in the bedroom and living room. Ashtrays were filled to overflow-ing with cigarette butts; some butts had fallen to the shabby wooden floors. Max had no carpeting, no rugs.

Jesse stood over the desk, catching a glimpse of Max's work.

"Away now," Max said sternly.

They sat down across from each other in the living room, Jesse on the couch, its innards squuushing out around him. Max lit a new cigarette and crossed his legs, placing a heavy marble ashtray at his feet.

"What can I do for you," he said, without a smile.

Jesse felt he had joined a stranger, that they were meeting for the first time, that all of their hours together had been a pose—Max had faked it for the gig. Probably the truth was: Max detested Jesse, a rich kid, a famous father, a wisenheimer, a lazy kid. This Max, here and now, was the true Max, able to speak out from his heart on his own turf, unafraid of Norman Savitt, furious that his writing had been interrupted. All those pages on the desk. The man was a genius.

"What can you do for me? I mean, what can *I* do for you?" Jesse said, wanting to regain Max. "How are you?" he asked, after a moment, feeling tears in his stomach.

"I'm unwell," Max said. "Just a bug, but I *am* writing."

"I'd love to see—"

"I'd prefer not. It has nothing whatsoever to do with you. The material is quite incomplete. I haven't shown it to anyone."

"What about your son?" Jesse asked.

Michael Bookstein scared Jesse. Little had been said or asked of him.

"We're not in touch," Max said.

"How come?"

"Michael belongs to his mother. I pay the bills for their conspiracy." Max took a drag from his cigarette.

Jesse felt joy. Michael Bookstein wasn't even in the picture. All this time, Jesse had secretly been wrestling with air. Max was his alone. "I don't get it," he said, getting it, wanting more of a good thing.

"Helen's point of view is, generally, that I am odious and uncompromising and impossible to deal with on the day to day of it. I'll admit to some of this. I'll admit to an exaggerated need for privacy. You, Jesse, are, in fact, the first person other than myself to set foot in here in over a year. Except for the cleaning lady, who, as you can tell, doesn't show up often. It's my work that counts, and though it may make me seem reclusive, it's my choice. Human commitment, one to the other, is far more spiritual than anything I can deal with. At the bottom, there's got to be faith as tough as a diamond, and I'm afraid I'm not the man for the job."

Max had a coughing spell. Jesse, across from him, took him in, in the heat, in the smoke, under the books. Bare feet, toenails uncut to the point of unsightliness, a surprising girth on a man too busy for meals. Jesse imagined the thousands of Goobers chocolate-coated peanuts in Max's middle, undigested, stored away, little sugar capsules in place for some lengthy hibernation down the road. Max's skin was sallow, his intense brown eyes were deep-set, enormous, and they crackled with intelligence. The overlooked mustache jumped wryly about, underlining a prominent nose, a hand-me-down from some small Russian town, shown up now on the musical face of a twentieth-century scholar, a voluminous man with frayed collars and wide yellow ties, hygienically unrealistic, alone. Jesse's geometry tutor had the answers. Everything was here in this beautiful, this *gorgeous* apartment. This was it.

"You know," Jesse said, "I wouldn't mind coming here for our lessons. You wouldn't have to go out of the house. I'd

take the Seventy-ninth Street crosstown bus and presto I'd
be here. And we could do it earlier, seven-thirty, right after
dinner. I wouldn't disturb a thing in here, you know."

"It's not a matter of that," Max said.

"What do you mean?" Jesse asked.

"What would your father have to say about it?"

"It never entered my mind," Jesse said. Which was true.

"With his permission, perhaps." Max's mustache was
agreeing to Jesse's plan. Max's eyes followed, softening.
Even after another coughing spell, Max's eyes remained
agreeable.

"In our spare time, could I go through some of the books?"
Jesse asked.

"What spare time do you have in mind," Max said.

"Max," Jesse said, "I give you my word of honor we'll find
spare time. Spare time is the *air*. You know?"

"We shall see what we shall see," Max said.

"Come on now, Max, don't go boring on me."

———————

"BECAUSE OF HIS books," Jesse replied to his father's question.
"After the geom session, then I can read a little. It's a real
library, Daddy. And it has good working space, and everything."

Jesse knew to stay clear of the truth: the dust, just about
everywhere; the two cartons of Heath bars and nothing else
in the refrigerator; the roaches in the bathroom, in the
kitchen, in the empty food cabinets; the *clank-clank* of the
radiators that bore holes into conversation; the closed windows and the heat and the smoke and the books under the
bed and behind the couch and the paperback books in the
medicine cabinet in the bathroom; and the piles of students'

papers flung far and wide, sticky from melted chocolate.

Was Max Bookstein a homo?

Norman Savitt never asked Jesse Savitt, never focused on it, though Jesse could feel it in his father's breathing.

Homo.

Not possible here. Max Bookstein displayed a heavy heterosexual heart, a long and winding road, a history with women, a son in college, a virile comportment. If Jesse had found a teacher *and* a friend, then 243 East Seventy-eighth Street wasn't too complicated a trip. Norman Savitt was almost confident.

In apartment 3A Jesse took to the masters. From the dust he pulled Flaubert and Hardy and Dostoevski. Sitting on Max's rotting couch, Jesse struggled with Virginia Woolf and Montaigne and Joyce and Nabokov. *Augie March* took his breath away.

From under the bed Jesse gathered periodicals. He had never held a literary periodical. He was fascinated and thrilled and wished to write something for one of them. Max told him that there wasn't any money in quarterlies. Jesse said that money wasn't the point.

Max's place. This was something!

Jesse asked Max what "perspicacious" meant. Max told him to look it up. Jesse looked up many words and wrote down their definitions. Jesse brought Heath bars and Goobers over to Max's house. He followed Max's rules: The study was off limits, out of bounds. Jesse could not use or answer Max's telephone. Jesse must be home no later than eleven. Saturday and Sunday afternoons were open-ended, reasonably. Jesse was not allowed in the place alone. Period.

In the spring, Jesse raised his geometry grades way above the passing mark. In celebration Max took him out to a bar. Jesse ordered a gin and tonic, Max had a beer.

"I'm making a list of books I'm going to read between now and June," Jesse said. "Will you give me advice?"

"Follow your instinct," Max said. "I'd rather you did it on your own. You have a good sense about you."

"I like it when we collaborate on things," Jesse said. "It's pleasurable."

"Is Proust on your list?"

"Did he really just shut himself away and do all that writing? Alone like that?"

"You ought to read something *about* him. There's an excellent biography by a man named Drummond."

"You seem to be a kind of Proust," Jesse said, sipping his drink.

"I'm a miniaturist, trapped in ignorance," Max said quietly. "My only dignity is that I know full well I'm not fooling anyone."

IN THE MONTH of May, Max told Jesse about Melissa Rhineheimer.

"It seems I have fallen in love," he said, on the phone.

Jesse expressed delight, but felt devastated. He asked about Melissa Rhineheimer. Max said she was a student at Hofstra, that absolutely no one on campus knew about it, that Melissa was "very pretty," that Melissa had "a poet's heart," that Melissa was twenty years old and wanted to be a writer. Jesse wished to know if she had ever been to Max's apartment. "Yes, three times," Max said. "Will I ever meet her?" Jesse asked. "In time," Max said. "For the moment, we're each other's secret."

That night Jesse lay awake, crushed by Melissa Rhineheimer's invasion. A very pretty girl with a poet's heart, lounging among the dust bunnies on Seventy-eighth Street, sharing the heat of Max's three little rooms, reading, *having been invited to read* Max's work in progress. A girl, surely of Jesse's own desire, out of reach under ordinary circumstances, wildly inaccessible in the lofty role of Max's intimate friend, Max's lover. *Lover.*

Max's sessions with Jesse were returned to Central Park West.

"I've got to give her some privacy," Max explained most gently.

"But when she's not there . . ." Jesse said.

"She's there, Jesse," Max said.

In the evening, once or twice, Jesse took the crosstown bus and hid in the shadows of Seventy-eighth Street, then in the courtyard below Max's window, hoping to catch a glimpse of Melissa and Max. Their sharing the letter "M" broke Jesse's heart. Their cohabitation, if that's what it was, stung Jesse's insides, as it took place right up there, behind that familiar, thrilling window, once Jesse's territory, now off limits, like Max's writing, like Max himself.

Jesse never saw them, Jesse could only imagine them, invisibly coming and going, sharing candy in the middle of the night, talking with each other in Max's steamy bedroom, planning for summer, for eternity, Jesse excluded, but spoken of nicely by Max, a kid he taught.

"Melissa would like to meet you," Max said, after Jesse's last exam at the end of the school year.

"Well, me too, for Christ's sake," Jesse said with a little chuckle, designed to underplay his interest, to reveal it only within the bounds of adultness.

"Why don't you drop by for a cocktail on Sunday afternoon," Max suggested.

"Come on, Max, you don't have a cocktail. Just Goobers is all you got." Another little knowing chuckle—we love each other, Max, and you can't fool me.

"You'd be surprised," Max said. "You *will* be surprised."

When Jesse showed up on Sunday afternoon, Melissa was out.

Max's apartment was immaculate. A new couch, an Oriental rug in the living room, carrots in the refrigerator, and cottage cheese and eggs and watermelon and oranges. And flowers in the bedroom, and a hosed-down bathroom, clean as can be, and brand-new towels.

"It's a castle, Max," Jesse said.

"Melissa," Max said with pride.

"Where is she?"

"She went to get tonic for your gin and tonic. I told her she didn't have to, but she insisted. She'll be back in a few minutes." Max lit a cigarette. "Sit down, sit down."

Jesse took a seat on the new couch, his old spot in the living room, his Colette spot, his Auden spot, polished up now, altered, removed from him forever. He waited on this Sunday in a waiting room for a gin and tonic, for the bits and pieces of Melissa Rhineheimer that she would permit him on the first visit. And look! Max's mustache was gone, revealing a younger man with light eyes.

"What happened to your mustache?" Jesse asked, knowing, understanding.

"It was a part of a costume I no longer cared for," Max said.

"But I saw you two weeks ago," Jesse said.

"It's new, it's new. I felt relieved when I was apprehended."

Melissa Rhineheimer entered the apartment with her own keys. "Hi," she said, standing in the threshold of the living room, holding a bag of groceries.

"Well, hi," Jesse said, standing, then sitting down immediately.

"I'll be in in a minute," she said, turning to the kitchen.

"She's young," Jesse said. And overweight, or so it seemed. A chunky girl with short brown hair, dressed in a plaid skirt and a white silk blouse. When she came back into the room and gave Jesse his drink, he noticed how pale she was, how fatigued she appeared. Jesse thought of the word "exhausted."

Melissa took a seat on the floor next to Max's chair and surrounded his left leg with her right arm.

"Max talks about you a lot," Melissa said.

"You, too," Jesse said, as if he had equal access to Max Bookstein. "So you're in Max's class?"

"You know, of course, that it would be very damaging if—"

"Of course," Jesse said. "I'm not about to say a word."

"I didn't mean—"

"No, I know you didn't. I mean—"

"You're not the issue," Max said. "We've just got to be inordinately discreet." He gave his lit cigarette to Melissa and reached for another.

Their sitting that way, Melissa attached to Max, sharing his cigarette, displaying their secret, made them, for Jesse, all the more conspiratorial and intimate. To retain any piece of Max, Jesse had to work at approving them, dazzling them with praise. Melissa's skirt, this new beige couch, the gin and tonic. Jesse became effusive.

"I can only say, and I mean this, that this house is just great. What you've *done* with Max's house."

"Max says you're a great reader. Max says *you* teach *him.*"

Had Max said that? Jesse wasn't sure and Max wasn't talking. Max sat there, pleased, smoking, feeling Melissa's arm around him, adored by both of these young people, in love with the girl, with her divine helplessness, her appetite for literature and physics, for what Max *knew.*

"This library, you know, is worth a fortune," Jesse said, continuing on, approving everything in sight.

"Milton, Virgil, Schopenhauer, Freud," Melissa said. "This is all I need." She inhaled deeply, an experienced smoking woman.

Jesse noticed that she didn't smile at all, that it would take quite a fandango to amuse this scholarly, sullen girl.

"We're going to spend the summer in Greece," Max said, out of the blue.

"Wow," Jesse said, knowing their trip would do him in. After the Acropolis, of what value could Jesse be? A C.I.T. in the Adirondacks, listening to Schenectady radio, hauling ten-year-olds to Fort Ticonderoga—a pointless and solitary summer. "May I write you?" he asked, seizing what he thought to be his only chance.

"By all means," Melissa said. "We'd be more than receptive."

"Greece," Jesse said respectfully.

"Have you traveled?" Melissa asked, resting her head on Max's leg.

"Not really. Not at all. I mean, California."

"Max and I are going to cover a lot of ground together," Melissa said. "I want to get him out of his routine."

"I understand," Jesse said. "I know you'll have a wonderful summer."

"Max is a very special man," Melissa said in a lowered voice.

"You're telling me," Jesse said with a smile.

DURING JULY AND August, Jesse wrote Max four letters, choosing his words carefully, conscious of Melissa Rhineheimer.

Near the end of the summer he received a postcard from London. "We've come to Great Britain to marry," Max had written in his elegant longhand. "Perfectly natural after two months in Greece, profoundly a secret. Thank you for your nice notes. We enjoyed them."

In the autumn Jesse dropped by at Seventy-eighth Street. He stayed an hour. Melissa and Max told him about the Greek islands, about their stop in Paris, about London. The best man had been a professor friend of Max's. They had toasted each other with ale after they got married.

Jesse studied alone, without benefit of a tutor. He called Max on January 2 to wish him a happy birthday. Max sounded preoccupied and curt.

In February Melissa called Jesse. She told him that Max had been terminated by Hofstra, and that he was in the hospital. Jesse went immediately to Sloan-Kettering, bearing Goobers peanuts and the *Saturday Review.*

"I swear, no one at the college knew," Max said, lying in bed under a sheet, sharing a semiprivate room with a man named Meltzer, who spoke on the phone in Yiddish all during Jesse's visit. "But this will give me a chance to finish my book."

He lay on his back, smoking a Camel cigarette, his mustache reinstated. "Oh, I tell you, Jesse, I'm not a spiritual man. I do think working alone will be good for me."

Jesse visited Max three more times. During the third visit, with Meltzer on the phone behind his yellow curtain, Max fell asleep.

In a little while, Max died in his sleep, and Jesse didn't know it. He had, in fact, closed his own eyes, numbed by Meltzer's rising, agitated voice.

A nurse came, then two doctors. Meltzer wanted to know what was going on.

ON THE THIRTIETH anniversary of Max Bookstein's death Jesse Savitt looked up his old friend in the phone book. Mrs. Max Bookstein was listed at 243 East Seventy-eighth Street. Jesse called the number. A woman answered. "Melissa?" Jesse said. "Yes?" the woman said. Jesse hung up.

CHLOE HUMMEL OF THE CHICAGO WHITE SOX

Jesse read seven newspapers a day. His father didn't discontinue their delivery, though he was leaving for four months to live in California to write songs for a film. Before he left, just after New Year's Day of 1956, he found a note from Jesse on his desk. Jesse had typed it, as he typed everything. He had taught himself to type when he was twelve, working at it for hours at a time, copying entire basketball schedules and baseball schedules, throwing away any page with a mistake. He had kept one page with what he felt to be a terrible mistake, and had pinned it to his bulletin board. Line thirty-five of sixty read: CLEVELAND AT DETROIT. Over this typo, in black crayon, he had scribbled: "I am a fool."

Now, five years after he had started, Jesse rarely made an error. His letters to Averell Harriman, Adlai Stevenson, Joseph Welch, Walter Lippmann, Mel Parnell; thank-you notes; shopping lists; the entire National Basketball Association schedule for the 1955–56 season—all these were impeccably produced on personal stationery. JESSE SAVITT, NEW YORK CITY is what suited him, up there on the top of each page. A citizen of the center of the world, a communicator. Even, Jesse felt, a commentator.

My Dear Daddy [Jesse had typed, under his extravagant banner], "I have come to rely heavily on your newspapers. They give me insights into things and keep me abreast of the times in which we live. I implore you not to stop them from coming, even though you will be living in another world with *The Hollywood Reporter* to see you through. I'd split the expense with you if you lent me the money to do this. It is very important to me, and I hope you'll take it under consideration.

Most Sincerely,
Your son Jesse

The seven New York papers continued on for Jesse, and for Marion.

To Marion Jesse rushed upon reception of a note from Averell Harriman. "Dear Mr. Savitt, I received your very constructive letter, and I am extremely pleased that you took the time to write it. You sound like a very intelligent young man."

To Marion Jesse rushed with a response from the president of the National Basketball Association. "Dear Mr. Savitt, Thank you for your suggestion. Your objection to an owner of one of our teams (Eddie Gottlieb of the Philadelphia Warriors) playing a role in planning the overall league schedule is without merit. Mr. Gottlieb offers his advice, as do others, during the long and sometimes tedious process of making out an equitable schedule for all franchises. Mr. Gottlieb is not biased in any way, nor are any other advisers who may or may not meet with me, or someone in the league office, from time to time. Nonetheless, I thank you for your suggestion that someone from the baseball world create our schedule. Sincerely, Maurice Podoloff."

To Marion Jesse rushed with Joseph Welch's letter. "You are very generous, sir, to recall my actions so long after the fact. You encourage me, and that is all, I think, that can be asked of a stranger."

"What am I going to do about Jesse?" Norman had asked his friend Lee Strasberg. "I don't want to take him out of school in the middle of his senior year. College is problematic, even without a disruption. What's he going to do in school in Los Angeles? I mean, I just can't do that to the boy."

"Why don't you find somebody to live with him," Strasberg had suggested. "There are any number of people at the Studio who would happily live up there with your son, just for the lodging of a penthouse. Someone responsible, who Jesse couldn't fool with."

Marion Hummel was an actress studying "with Lee." "Lee says that sometimes the best course of action is no action." "Being with Lee is unworldly." "Lee goes directly to the center, and all of us with Lee know that about him." So said Marion Hummel during her first talk with Jesse.

They sat in Norman's living room, meeting. Norman wandered in and out, with his ears open.

"You understand that the Actors Studio is a school of acting—that is, a school of thought *about* acting. I happen to believe in it with all my heart. I tell you, Lee Strasberg is an extraordinary man. I've studied with him for two years, so he knows me pretty well."

Marion Hummel, Lee Strasberg's recommendation, was a tall twenty-seven-year-old woman from Chicago. She was living in a fifth-floor walk-up on West Forty-seventh Street, and the prospect of spending four months in a penthouse, surrounded by a terrace, with the son of Norman Savitt, and with all those records, all that music, while bringing in a hundred and fifty dollars a week simply to chaperone a seventeen-year-old, while still going to the Studio, still in Lee's classes, and still auditioning, still out there in the theater—everything about the plan attracted Marion Hummel.

"What if you get a job out of town?" Norman asked, passing through the living room.

"Couldn't we cross that bridge when we come to it?" Marion replied quietly. "I mean, it seems unlikely, doesn't it?"

Everything about Marion was quiet. Her eyes were hazel, her gaze steady, unflirtatious, kind. All of her face came to a point: a lantern chin, a thorough straight nose, even her temples and cheekbones seemed to thrust themselves undemandingly forward. Her eyes, set a bit too close together, had created a character actress rather than an ingenue, though Marion's light brown hair did shimmer in the sun from the terrace and her delicate hands did rest most gracefully in her lap. She had muscular legs from years of dancing, and an unhurried gait coming into the room. She spoke slowly, somewhat haltingly, taking her time, never wishing to inflict damage of even the most minute kind. The theater of her life had placed the sound of her voice directly on the ethnic fence, without geographical material with which she could be identified, or brashness or unguided enthusiasm in the upper register. Everything about her face crinkled when she laughed, something that Jesse immediately found he could effect. They were companions at once, as Jesse's father accurately observed when he called Lee Strasberg to thank him for Marion Hummel.

The day his father left, Jesse rode out to the airport with him. "I want to say good-bye at Idlewild, not in a doorway," he told Norman.

The January morning was clear, icy cold. Jesse, bundled up, helped his father load the taxi.

"You think you'll need all those sweaters you packed?" Jesse asked.

"It gets chilly everywhere at this time of year," Norman said. "Besides, I like sweaters."

"Who's to stop you," Jesse said, with a laugh.

"What do you truly think of Marion?" Norman asked as they started out.

"She's a gasser," Jesse said. "She'll be a lot of fun. I can teach her about politics, she can teach me about the theater."

"That's true," Norman said. "And, you know, at all times I'm a phone call away."

"And that you'll come back now and then?"

"And that I'll come back. I don't know the exact dates, but I'll be back and forth, just as I said."

"If Max were alive it wouldn't be so savaging," Jesse said.

"Savaging is not the right word, Jesse boy. Sometimes you pick out overly dramatic language, so that it distorts everything."

"What's wrong with savaging?"

"Your dad is taking a job for four months. A pleasant lady will be living with you. You've got your school schedule, you've got an allowance—"

"I've got my correspondence," Jesse said.

"That, too," Norman said. "The point is, savaging means, well, to savage."

"To create misery," Jesse said.

"Am I creating misery for you?" Norman asked.

"Of course not," Jesse said. "Can we talk often?"

"A hundred times a day."

"What if sometimes it's necessary?"

"Then it's necessary, that's all there is to it."

At Idlewild, Jesse helped his father unload the taxi. He hugged him good-bye.

"Jesse boy," Norman said, "be kind to people. Be fair."

"I know what you mean," Jesse replied, "and I'll do my best to bring it off."

"Here's money for the cab back, and something extra," Norman said, slipping fifty dollars to his son.

"I'll spend it wisely and well," Jesse said.

"You're a good little actor," Norman said, draping his arm around Jesse's shoulder.

"In that case, Marion and I will get along fantastically. I'll really learn from her."

———

MARION MADE JESSE's dinner every night at a quarter of seven. She read and praised his long letters to public figures.

"You sure believe in what you're doing," she said.

"One has to believe in what one does," Jesse replied wisely. "Nothing comes from nothing," he continued. "Progress comes from believing."

Marion cleaned up after Jesse, straightening his room while he was at school, though a maid came regularly to attend to such things.

Marion listened to Jesse play the piano. His father's songs were always at the top of his list.

" 'Over the purple hills, far away, far far away,' " Jesse sang.

"He wanted to write a cowboy kind of song," he explained to Marion and several other actors who had gathered in Norman's living room to rehearse a scene for Lee. Instead, the young man of the house allowed them a bit of Norman's catalog.

"That's really good," Marion said, sitting on the couch between a young man and an older woman.

"You've got yourself quite a talented dad," Jesse was told

by an actor named Marty Brandon, who had actually stood by the piano during "Over the Purple Hills."

"He writes both words and music," Brandon said. "There aren't many guys who did that. Berlin and Porter, and who else?"

"Frank Loesser," Jesse said, getting up from the piano. "But he started out as just a lyric writer, so he doesn't count entirely."

"And no one else," Brandon went on. He was a short red-haired man, perhaps twenty-five. "I love Broadway music. I always wished I could sing, but I'm an actor instead."

"In writing for the theater you've got to move the story forward, if it's possible," Jesse said, standing a few feet from the piano. "It's not like the old days, when songs were just thrown in for no reason."

"You're really lucky," Brandon said. "I mean, brought up in this family."

"Family," Jesse replied absently, preparing to leave the room, sensing the other's impatience.

"I mean it, you're really lucky," Brandon said again.

"There's more than luck involved," Jesse said. "You've got to want to learn about all of it, or, otherwise, what good is it?"

"I JUST LIKE to pretend I'm someone else," Marion was telling Jesse, sitting at the foot of his bed, saying good night. "Being, being imaginary, is very exciting to me. I can live in another century, I can eclipse my own self. Do you know what I mean?"

"You mean, do *better* than yourself?" Jesse asked, dressed in pajamas, the covers pulled up to his chin.

"Better? Do I mean better?" Marion wondered out loud. "No, not necessarily better. It's that I could create another being who knew different things, things *I* don't know. You learn about what a character knows in the way you work in a scene, or when you're working with a whole text. You get to know the material of that person's life, that person's circumstances."

"I want to be a writer, to be able to do what you're talking about," Jesse said. "I like to go into corners and find out stuff. Please don't misunderstand me, I don't mean incriminating stuff. I mean stuff about other people's lives, secret stuff, but not savage stuff."

"Well, then you know what I'm talking about," Marion said, getting up from the bed. "You and I want to do the same thing," she added.

"Make up stuff," Jesse said.

"I guess," Marion said.

"You think that's too gross?"

"I don't think it's gross, do you? I think it's, well, admirable, in a way."

"But what about wanting to snoop," Jesse said. "Sometimes, right when I'm snooping, I'm thinking, You're a snoop."

"Give in to it, Jesse," Marion said, standing in his doorway. "You say you want to be a writer. That's just like saying you want to be a snoop. Do you get what I mean?"

———————

JESSE FOUND A letter from Marion to her sister Chloe in Chicago.

"You'll really like Jesse," she had written, in green ink, dated February 5, the day before. "He has a lot of ideas and he's full of pep, and though he can be moody, basically he's fun to be with. Just come and make yourself at home. Stay a few days, or whatever. There's a folding bed in the study that's all yours."

At dinner, Jesse told Marion that he had read her letter to Chloe.

"Why did you do that?" Marion asked without anger.

"I didn't really read it, I just glanced at it," he said.

"Did you learn anything?"

"That Chloe's coming here."

"Is that all right? Just for a few days? She's a great girl. She's an actress in Chicago with the Turtle Bay Players."

"Sure, it's OK," Jesse said. "She's not negative, is she?"

"Chloe? Negative? Now, that's a laugh," Marion said, dishing out more of her lasagna to them both.

"Is she older or younger than you?"

"She's twenty-two, and she's my best friend. She says that Chicago is freezing and that New York would be a relief."

"And she's not morose? I'm susceptible to moroseness."

"She's the opposite, I promise. Try her on for size."

On the phone, Jesse told his father about Chloe.

"If she's anything like Marion, she'll be a joy," Norman said, from Beverly Hills.

"She's exactly like Marion," Jesse said.

"How do you know?" Norman asked.

"Marion said so. She said they're like twins."

"Great," Norman said.

"Daddy, I got a letter from Senator Kefauver today."

"Terrific! What did he say?"

"He just thanked me for my support, which I really hadn't offered. He interpreted my letter incorrectly."

"But he responded, as they all do," Norman said enthusiastically.

"What if I wrote *you* a letter. Would you respond?" Jesse asked.

"Naturally I'd respond. You've never really ever written me anything, except from camp. I'd love to hear from you."

"Well then, maybe, after Chloe leaves, I'll write you about her visit," Jesse said.

"I'll look forward to that," Norman said. "You want to hear a great melody?" he asked.

"Sure, I do," Jesse said.

"Wait a minute, I'll bring the phone to the piano," Norman said.

This was nothing new to Jesse. Often, Norman moved phones around, tugging them over to pianos.

He played a few chords.

"Can you hear me OK?" he asked.

"Perfect," Jesse said.

A waltz came floating out from Beverly Hills. A waltz in a minor key.

"Oh, Daddy, that's beautiful!" Jesse said, feeling great pride.

"You liked it? Honestly?"

"It's something really new," Jesse said, watching snow begin to build outside his window.

"I was shooting for something distinctive," Norman said.

"Play it again," Jesse said.

Norman played it three times.

Jesse hummed it back to him.

"You really like it?" Norman asked, with a gay and hopeful tone familiar to his son.

"Absolutely," Jesse said. "I'll sing it for Chloe when she gets here. It'll win her confidence."

"Even though it's a waltz in a nonwaltz age?"

"Oh, Daddy, you're wrong. It just depends on the particular waltz."

WHEN CHLOE ARRIVED, Jesse was at home, alone.

She stood in the hall wearing gloves and a scarf.

"Brrr," she said.

"I'm Jesse," he said.

"You're taller than I thought," Chloe said, still standing in the hall.

"Come in," Jesse said. "Let me take you," he added.

"Thank you for the invitation," Chloe said, standing in the study where she would sleep, unraveling her scarf, taking off her gloves. "Oh, my," she said, "what a gorgeous house."

Chloe kept taking things off. She took off what looked to Jesse like a man's tweed jacket. She removed galoshes, shoes, and a pair of sweat socks. She took barrettes out of her red hair, allowing it to fall to her shoulders. She took off a long-sleeved shirt and a plaid skirt, which left her in black long-sleeved leotards.

"I am beat," she said, falling onto the Castro that Marion had prepared as a bed.

Chloe had clear white skin and wide blue eyes. She couldn't have been more than a hundred pounds, Jesse thought, his eyes stuck helplessly on her remarkable bosom.

"You like my breasts, I see," Chloe said, turning Jesse's face to crimson.

"Why be embarrassed," Chloe said, getting up, putting an arm around him and kissing him on the cheek. "I'm the one who's the freak."

"You're not a freak," Jesse hastened to tell her. "You don't have the correct idea."

"I have every correct idea," Chloe said cheerfully. "I'm just about five feet, and I have ridiculously big breasts, and a gorgeous body, and I'll just have to learn to live with it."

"Them," Jesse pointed out, and quickly added, "I'm sorry, I didn't wish to be arrogant."

But Chloe was laughing. "You're so sweet," she told him, slapping his backside. "You know what I'd like? A cup of coffee and a cigarette."

Chloe, barefoot, followed Jesse to the kitchen.

In a few moments, Jesse, who disliked coffee, accepted his cup from Chloe's long white fingers.

"Black?" she asked.

"Of course," Jesse said.

"Do you smoke?" Chloe asked, sitting down at the kitchen table.

"I used to, but I don't anymore."

"How could you *used* to. What are you, seventeen?"

"I took it up as an affectation," Jesse said truthfully. "But it just made me feel sick, so I stopped."

"Good for you," she said. "I wish I could. I'm a pack-a-day girl if ever there was one." Chloe laughed, as if she had told a joke, crossing her legs, taking a sip of her own black coffee, her hair falling into her face.

Her amazing red hair.

"You make good coffee," Jesse said.

"I'm good around the house. That's why Marion invited me."

"That's not true. She really wanted to see you," Jesse said.

"We love each other. We're good sisters. Both actresses, can you imagine?" Another big laugh from Chloe.

"Have you been in anything?" Jesse asked.

"A couple of things in Chicago. Whew, it's cold in Chicago."

"You haven't come to Miami, you know."

"And I made a film," Chloe continued.

"Which one?" Jesse asked excitedly.

"It's a risqué film," Chloe said, "done on a shoestring in Las Vegas."

"I don't happen to know what risqué means," Jesse said, knowing full well what risqué meant, wanting Chloe to define it, to define herself in it. He would be off the hook, not having asked a thing.

"How refreshing!" Chloe said, catching his eyes with her own fabulous blue eyes. "Someone who admits he doesn't know what a certain word means. I mean, everybody *I* know pretends to know all kinds of words. They just go uh-huh, when a word comes out, as if they knew what it meant. You don't go un-huh. That's refreshing." She took another sip of coffee and a drag of her cigarette.

"What does it mean, though, risqué?" Jesse asked, keeping her in tow.

"It kind of means off-color. Un-Disney-like."

"What do you mean?"

"Well, I'm like, nude. But only in a certain scene."

"Well, that's great, isn't it?" Jesse said.

"Of course it is. I'm a beautiful girl, and those are sexy scenes."

"Scenes?" Jesse said.

"Two, that's all."

"Has anyone ever seen them?" Jesse asked.

"Not around here," Chloe told him, hushing her voice. "And don't you *dare* tell Marion."

"I give you my solemn word," Jesse said.

"Otherwise, I'll never tell you anything else."

"Chloe Hummel, you can count on me," Jesse said, taking her hand across the table, shaking it gravely. "It's our bond," he told her quietly.

"Here's to our bond," Chloe said, clinking her coffee cup with his, in a toast, forcing him into another sip, cementing their unexpected conspiracy.

"MY SISTER'S NEAT," Chloe said, lounging full length on a living room couch, wearing only a terry-cloth robe, her hair still wet after a shower.

"You've always been the so-called neat one," Marion said, addressing Chloe, but pulling Jesse into it with a brief shift of her eyes. She was sitting next to him on the smaller couch on the other side of the coffee table.

"Well, I meant neat meaning terrific. You're the terrific one, I'm the black sheep."

"Never a black sheep," Marion said.

"But look at me," Chloe said, extending her arms, as if concluding a song. "Look at me," she repeated. "Where did this red hair come from? And this freaky body? Nobody else in our family has red hair, or anything."

"I think that's a misuse of the word 'anything,'" Jesse said, protecting Marion.

"Oh, you mean as far as attributes are concerned," Chloe said, discovering Jesse's meaning. "It isn't that nobody else has no attributes."

"Of course not, silly," Marion said.

"But wouldn't you say, Marion, wouldn't you say that I've always been different? Just a little out of the way?"

"Out of the way?" Marion said. "Never out of the way. Always right in the center of things."

"The center of things," Chloe said. And then, impressing upon Jesse the oddball sense of it: "If you're *the* center of things, you're out of the way. Different. Because there's no other center of things. You see what I mean?"

"That's what we call Chloe logic," Marion said, getting up to go to the kitchen. "Anyone want any fruit?"

"No thank you, ma'am," Jesse said.

"You got any ice cream?" Chloe said.

"Schrafft's chocolate," Marion replied, from the hall.

"Bring me the container," Chloe said. "And a spoon," she added, in a bit of a shout.

"How do you stay so thin?" Jesse inquired as conversationally as he could manage.

"It's my metabolism. I can eat a hundred pounds of chocolate ice cream and actually lose weight."

"That's amazing," Jesse said.

"I've always been that way. Different. You see what I mean?" Chloe tucked her legs under her.

"Well, it's amazing."

"Thank you," Chloe said, running her hands through her slowly drying hair. "You're not built so bad yourself."

Jesse was shocked, and unable to reply. Until that moment, no one—no man, woman, or child on the face of the earth—had ever passed a remark that spoke of his body. Good or bad wasn't the issue. It was simply his bodily being that had gone unaddressed.

Jesse knew of his own aliveness. He had observed his puberty and other remarkable events. He had dropped the idea of his own invisibility a few years earlier when it became apparent that he *was* visible to other people, who spoke sentences in his direction; the every day of it, the pass-the-salt of it. He wasn't Harvey the rabbit, or Topper, or any other see-through item. Now, here was this Chloe, not only commenting on his actual presence but throwing a compliment his way. *He wasn't built so bad himself.* In other words, he wasn't a fat jerk, he wasn't distorted, he wasn't—and here he spoke the word to Chloe in a disengaged blurt— "Freaky."

"You think you're freaky?" Chloe said.

"No. I was just thinking that you don't think I'm freaky."

"Shit no," Chloe said. "I think you're sexy."

"You think he's sexy?" Marion said, returning with Chloe's ice cream and a peach for herself.

"Don't you?" Chloe said.

"Do I think you're sexy, Jesse?" Marion said, giving Chloe her quart of Schrafft's. "I don't think of you as sexy, but I think you're a good-looking young man. Chloe's a weasel. She finds sex in everything."

"Is that so bad?" Chloe said.

"That's what she's been saying all her life," Marion told Jesse. " 'Is that so bad.' That's a Chloeism."

"If ever there was one," Chloe said, most pleased at the very idea of Chloeisms. "And do you know what another Chloeism is?" she continued. " 'If ever there was one.' I say it all the time."

Jesse felt uncomfortable with this. He tried to figure out why. Did Chloe make up Chloeisms to create the character of Chloe Hummel? Is that what she meant? And if that's what she meant, wouldn't it have been better to have kept it to herself? On the other hand, he reasoned, maybe *not* keeping it to herself was the ultimate Chloeism, which made for a charming girl, not . . . not what? Ah, thought Jesse, not a fake.

"I made a film," Chloe was saying to Marion.

"In Chicago?" Marion asked, taking a bite of her peach.

"In Las Vegas," Chloe replied, surprising Jesse with this revelation. After all, they had made a pact.

"What's it about?" Marion asked.

"It's about Jesus, or something. I don't know, it was just a bit part. I was a nun."

"Why shoot a movie about Jesus in Vegas?" Marion asked.

"Because of the climate," Chloe said, an explanation that seemed satisfactory to one and all.

"You know, we're going to have a snowstorm," Jesse said.

"Not a storm so much," Marion said. "I thought I heard something about an inch or two."

"But it's from the northeast," Jesse said. "And those things are unpredictable. As a matter of fact, I predict more than an inch or so."

"So do I," Chloe said gaily.

"Why do you think that?" Marion asked her sister.

"Because Jesse thinks it, and I think he knows certain things. I think he's sophisticated."

"Thank you," Jesse said, allowing the pleasure of Chloe's compliments to wash through him.

"Do you know that Jesse keeps in touch with world-famous figures?" Marion said, gesturing respectfully in his direction.

"Like who?" Chloe asked, stretching full length again, her arms behind her head.

"Tell her," Marion said to Jesse. "He writes to them, and they respond."

"Adlai Stevenson, for one," Jesse said. "Need I go on?"

"Please do," Chloe said enthusiastically.

"Georgia Gibbs, the singer. And do you know who Red Smith is? He's a sportswriter. And Jerry Coleman. He's a baseball player."

"Yankee second baseman," Chloe said. "And shortstop, too, on occasion."

"How did you know that?" Jesse said, falling in love for good right then and there.

"I'm a baseball fan, a White Sox fan. They win ninety-one games, they still finish third. Two fifteen-game winners, one thirteen-game winner, and an eleven-game winner, and they still finish third."

"You sure are a White Sox fan," Jesse said, immersed in Chloe, overwhelmed by Chloe. He wanted to take her robe off. He didn't know what he wanted to do after that. Certainly some kind of kissing, and real holding.

Marion was saying something like: Chloe's been a baseball fan all her life, she really knows the game.

But Jesse was long gone, out of hearing range, though he remained seated next to Marion.

"So you like my sister?" Marion said, tapping Jesse's knee affectionately.

"Is there anything *not* to like?" Jesse said, with a severity that made Marion withdraw her hand.

"Some people hate me," Chloe said with a smile.

"I don't know who they could be," Jesse said.

"Chloe's exaggerating," Marion said. "She was always very popular. I'm five years older, and I saw it happen. I was always jealous of her, until we became real friends, about, when was it, six or seven years ago? Wouldn't you say that's when we became really good friends?"

"Yeah, I think so, but I was never jealous of you before," Chloe said.

"There's a Chloeism," Marion said. "As if she had anything to be jealous about."

"Let's get down to brass tactics," Chloe said, sitting up. "You were always the queen, the actress, the success of the family. You're in the *Studio,* for Christ's sake. *I'd* never get into the Studio. I'm not talented enough for those guys, for big Mr. Lee Strasberg. You're the winner in the family, and I've never been jealous." Chloe lay back again, and folded her hands on her stomach.

"That's nice of you to say," Marion said. "You see why I love my sister?" she said to Jesse.

"Yes," Jesse replied, in a brand-new kind of whisper. He heard the whisper himself, and felt embarrassed by it. *Something out of his own mouth in someone else's voice.*

"I think you've won Jesse over," Marion pointed out to Chloe.

"He's just impressed with my baseball," Chloe said.

"No, you're all wrong," Jesse said. "What you said about Marion is true about you. You're neat. Honestly. So is Marion, but just different neat."

"I'm not meant to be neat," Marion said softly.

"Don't be silly," Chloe said.

"I agree with Chloe," Jesse said, wishing to speak her name. "Chloe is right, you're just silly. Chloe loves you."

"We love each other," Marion said, smiling at them both.

"That's what Chloe said before you got home. Just that."

"You got any Oreos?" Chloe asked. "It would be great if you had Oreos."

"We do, and I'll get them," Jesse said.

"And a glass of milk," Chloe said as Jesse got up.

"You sure have some appetite," Jesse said.

"I'm the biggest eater, if ever there was one," Chloe said.

———

IN THE MIDDLE of the night Jesse was awakened by Marion.

"I'm hurting," she moaned, taking her usual place at the foot of his bed.

Startled, Jesse sat up.

"I'm hurting," Marion said.

"Are you in pain?" Jesse asked.

"Terrible," Marion said, holding her belly.

"Where, show me where," Jesse said, getting out of bed and turning on the light.

"Right here," Marion said, pointing.

"I think that's where the appendix is," Jesse said. "There was a kid in class. Did you ever have your appendix out?"

"No," Marion said, obviously frightened by Jesse's diagnosis.

"I think that's what this is," Jesse said.

"Oh God," Marion said.

"What time is it?"

"I don't know. Three-thirty," Marion told him. "Jesse, I'm hurting."

"We're going to the hospital," he said, grabbing his clothes and disappearing into the bathroom.

"I don't wanna go to the hospital," Marion said.

"Tough," Jesse said. "Get dressed fast," he ordered, sticking his head out the bathroom door.

Marion did as he said, swaying down the hall to her room, doubled over.

"Should we tell Chloe?" Marion asked when they were ready.

"Let her sleep," Jesse said.

On the street, Marion said, "Jesus, the snow."

"I was right," Jesse said.

"This isn't an inch or two," Marion said, her eyes showing panic.

"We'll get you there," Jesse said, guiding them east, across Eighty-ninth Street.

"Where are we going?" Marion asked, when they finally reached Lexington Avenue.

"Doctors Hospital. The best hospital in the world."

"Where is it?" Marion asked, her mouth frozen around her words.

"Over there," Jesse said, not telling her precisely the truth. "Come on, Marion, keep moving."

"I'm hurting," she said, beginning to cry.

Jesse held his arm tightly around her.

The snow, in a constant whirl, blew ferociously into their faces.

"I'm gonna die," Marion said.

"You're not going to die," Jesse said, knowing that they would make it somehow.

Numb with cold, they stumbled into the emergency room of Doctors Hospital.

Marion was attended to rapidly: appendicitis, no time to lose.

Jesse sat in a waiting room, flipping through several issues of *Life* magazine and thinking of Chloe. Chloe, who knew all about Jerry Coleman, and the Chicago White Sox. Minnie Minoso, Billy Pierce, Dick Donovan, Sherm Lollar, Nellie Fox, Jungle Jim Rivera, the whole White Sox picture. She had the big picture, the overview. She was so beautiful. She was so *bright*. So very, very bright. So spontaneous, and even-tempered. So perfect.

Jesse lost all thought of Marion.

Later, a surgeon materialized with good news. Everything had gone satisfactorily. Miss Marion Hummel was OK. Currently she was in the recovery room. She would be in the hospital nine or ten days. She was a brave woman. And she was fine.

Jesse had lost track of time. When he went outside the hospital, he was surprised to find that it was morning, though the storm raged on.

A cab pulled up, skidding a little in the snow. Jesse rode home in the luxury of its warmth, caught in reveries of Chloe Hummel. Chloe, who had slept through everything, was probably still sleeping, sleeping in his very own house, her red hair spread over everything.

Chloe Hummel, of the Chicago White Sox.

JESSE HAD BEEN right, Chloe was dead asleep, lying on her back with a quilt pulled only to her belly. She was wearing a cotton nightie with daisies everywhere: up and down the arms, across the white collar, across the phenomenal bosom.

Jesse stood for many minutes, peering in at her, having eased her door open just a bit to have a look. Had he been caught, his excuse was simple: Marion's in the hospital, and I had to tell you.

But Chloe was out of it, her mouth slightly open, her face in repose the face of an adolescent girl, guileless and un-menacing. He wondered if she woke up slowly, cranky and whiny on the way to caffeine. Or did Chloe Hummel bound into personality, as if sleep had been but a semicolon?

Jesse waited until nine to call his father; it was 6 A.M. in California.

A woman's voice answered.

"Is Norman Savitt there," Jesse asked.

"Who's calling," the woman said.

"His son."

"Is this Jesse?" the woman asked.

"Yes," Jesse replied.

"Well, hello there. I've heard so much about you. I'm a friend of your dad. I'll wake him."

Jesse heard some shuffling around, perhaps a hand over the receiver—he wasn't sure through the long-distance hiss.

"Jesse boy, everything OK?" Norman said at once.

"The thing is, Marion's had her appendix taken out," Jesse said. "I took her to Doctors Hospital. They said she's going to be fine."

"What happened?"

"She got sick in the middle of the night, and she was in pain, so I took her to Doctors Hospital and they said it was her appendix, and so she had an operation, and I waited over there until it was over, and the guy said she was fine, and she'll be there nine or ten days, and then she'll come home and she'll be fine. We're having a snowstorm."

"I heard about the snow. Is there anything you want me to do?" Norman asked.

"Maybe send her flowers, or something like that," Jesse said, hearing movement down the hall, thinking that Chloe was awake.

"I will, I will, that's a good idea. Is her sister there?"

"Yes, fortunately. Chloe. She's just like Marion. Very considerate. We'll do fine."

"How are you doing otherwise?" Norman asked.

"I'm doing great," Jesse said.

"I've written a *great* love song," Norman said.

"What's it called?" Jesse asked, always ready for the new song, with or without Chloe Hummel.

"It's called 'On the Other Hand.' It's sung by a woman in the story who's torn between two men, and in the lyric, which I haven't finished yet, she considers the pros and cons of each of the men. It goes, 'On the one hand, he'll have money in the bank, that's something to be thankful for, but on the other hand'—and then she'll sing about the other fellow. You follow me? And the bridge'll go something like:

'A tug of war goes on inside of me; it's the safe and sane against the wild and free.' Something like that."

"It's wonderful," Jesse said. "Can you play it for me?"

"I'm not near the piano now. You know it's six in the morning, don't you?"

"But I had to tell you about Marion," Jesse said.

"I understand completely. It's just that I'm in another room. I'll call you and play it for you later today. I can't wait for you to hear it. And it fits the screenplay."

"Wonderful, Daddy," Jesse said.

"You think you'll be OK with Marion's sister?"

"I know I will. She's very responsible," Jesse said.

"Are you going to school today?" Norman asked.

"I'm on the way. I'll be late, but I've got an excuse, don't you think?"

"If they cause any trouble, *I'll* deal with them," Norman said with a laugh in his voice.

"Well, OK, Daddy," Jesse said.

"I can hear you growing up," Norman said.

"Stop it, Daddy," Jesse said angrily.

"Let your old man make a comment or two every now and then."

At that moment Chloe came into the room in her nightie, sleepy-eyed and dazed.

"Sure," Jesse said to Norman.

"I'm proud of you, that's all. Can't a father be proud of his son?"

"Sure," Jesse said, feeling Chloe's good-morning hand on his back.

When Norman was finally gone, off the line, safe and sound in California, with some kind of woman, Jesse turned to Chloe to announce the news.

"Chloe," he started, "Marion's in the hospital. Nothing

serious. Her appendix had to be taken out, and she's in great shape."

"Where is she?" Chloe asked.

"Doctors Hospital," Jesse said.

"Where's that?" Chloe asked.

"It's way over on the east side."

"How did she get there?" Chloe asked intensely.

"I walked her there," Jesse said.

"In this snow?"

"Yes, in this snow. I had no other choice. No cabs, no nothing. It was four in the morning, or something."

"Why didn't you wake me up?" Chloe asked, with no discernible irritation.

"What could you have done except freeze your ass off. I mean, you came here to get out of the Chicago cold, and you'd have been walking something like eight *long* blocks in a blizzard."

"Thoughtful," Chloe said, putting her arm around Jesse's waist.

"I'm sure she's sleeping now," Jesse said.

"Should we visit her?" Chloe asked.

"Of course," Jesse said. "But later. I mean, the snow. Look at it on the terrace. That's a foot of snow out there, at the very least, and it's still coming down."

"Maybe we should call her. What does the appendix do in the body?"

"Nothing. That's why it's called the appendix. It's a useless thing. When it gets infected or flamed up, then you have to have it out. No big deal," Jesse said reassuringly.

"I'm afraid of hospitals," Chloe said. "You want coffee?"

"Have you ever had an operation?" Jesse asked, on the way to the kitchen.

"Never, are you kidding?"

Chloe opened the refrigerator to look around.

"There's beef stew in there," Jesse said, thinking of his own breakfast.

"Hey, do you see what I see?" Chloe said, beckoning Jesse to her side.

"What," Jesse asked, looking at everything in the refrigerator.

"What are you, blind?" Chloe asked, with mischief in her voice.

"Grapefruit juice?" Jesse said helplessly.

"Hey, kiddo, take a look at the champagne," Chloe said.

"In the morning?" Jesse said.

Chloe stood straight up and faced him.

"There are certain mornings when the goblins are sleeping. Champagne mornings. They're the best." Chloe actually giggled, an inoffensive little chuckle of a thing, on the safe side of coyness.

"Are the goblins sleeping?" Jesse asked, more coy than Chloe, Jesse's first incautious step.

"This is a day for them to sleep through, if ever there was one," Chloe said, removing the champagne from the top shelf.

"It's my father's champagne," Jesse said, without any conviction at all.

"But it's snowing, little man," Chloe said. "Where oh where are the glasses. In here?" she said, pulling open a cabinet door. "In here?" she said, pulling open a cabinet door. "In here?" she said, opening another. "Ah," she said triumphantly, "look what I've found!"

"A CALIFORNIA CHAMPAGNE," Chloe noted after a sip or two.

"Does it make a difference?" Jesse asked.

"I would have expected French, Piper Heidsieck, or something. But this is good. It's dry."

Chloe finished her champagne quickly, and poured more. Jesse followed, doing as she did.

Then he wanted to read her a letter he had written to J. D. Salinger.

"Did you ever come across any Salinger material?" he asked.

"I read *Catcher in the Rye*, is that it?"

"It's *'The' Catcher in the Rye,*" Jesse replied, sitting beside her on the long green living room couch, her feet in his lap.

He squeezed one of her ankles and got up, returning in a moment with a lengthy typewritten letter.

"Why do you paint your toenails pink?" he asked, sitting back down, once again taking her feet in his lap.

"Don't you think they're rather gay?" she laughed, pointing at them with her glass.

"Certainly they're gay," Jesse said.

"But," Chloe said.

"No but, they're gay."

"But you don't like them?"

"They're Chloe," Jesse said.

"Aren't they, though," she said.

"I'll only read you just a little. Are you ready?" Jesse said, glancing her way.

"As ready as I'll ever be," Chloe said.

" 'Dear Mr. Salinger,' " Jesse began, taking another look at Chloe to ensure her attention.

" 'Dear Mr. Salinger,' " Jesse repeated. " 'Having read and reread your story, "Raise High the Roof Beam, Carpenters," I wanted to make some contact with you, even though it may turn out to be a one-sided contact, in view of what I understand is your unbending rule not to answer fan mail or to correspond with strangers or in fact have anything to do with anyone. My understanding of your need for privacy is profound, such is my own need for privacy and my lack of it. I too have a very large family, just like your own Glass family—' Chloe, I'm making this part up, about a large family and all. And also, the Glass family is a family he's writing about."

"I see," Chloe said, sipping champagne.

" 'I too have a very large family, just like your own Glass family, which deprives me in large measure of personal privacy. There is always such clamor in the house, and lots of accusations, the kind of accusations that the Glass family doesn't make. All of this is by way of telling you, or trying to tell you, how wonderful your story is. It is a masterful display of a great writer at work. It is sensitive to little things, and at the same time to dreadful human behavior. Its last line, about a blank piece of paper being sent by way of explanation, is a masterpiece of conclusion.' "

"That's beautifully written on your part," Chloe said. " 'A masterpiece of conclusion.' You're a real writer."

"I don't need to continue," Jesse said. "The rest of the letter just deals with Zen, which is a kind of religion, and then there's an evaluation of his oeuvre, up to now."

"What's oeuvre?" Chloe asked. "You see, I'm not afraid to ask when I don't know something."

"An oeuvre is a man's body of work, his whole output," Jesse explained, rubbing her feet, letting his letter slide to the floor.

"You know what my oeuvre is?" Chloe asked with a smile. "The film in Vegas, and a couple of little rinky-dink parts with the Turtle Bay Players in Chicago. It's not even an oeuvre, it's an ooo."

Jesse laughed. "That's more than my oeuvre," he said.

"My oeuvre is a bunch of letters to strangers. So you're way ahead of me."

"But I'm, what, I'm five years older than you. I would have to have done something, for Christ's sake."

"Someday I'll have an oeuvre. Marion says I'm a snoop, because I read other people's secret stuff. I mean, she's not angry or anything. She just thinks that a reporter—that's what I want to be—a reporter is a natural-born snoop. That's how I found out you were coming. I read it in a letter Marion wrote to you."

"That's exciting," Chloe said. "It's, like, even erotic."

"What do you mean by that?" Jesse asked.

"Just kind of snooping around, picking up clues in secret, all that stuff. Secret is actually erotic. I mean, the potential is so great."

"The potential for what?" Jesse said, feeling that he was leading her forward.

"Well, you know, for hidden things, like sex things. Who's sleeping with who; pictures, stuff, secret stuff."

"I guess," Jesse said, not so surefooted with the turn of events. Reading his letter to Salinger was one thing; talking about sex out loud was quite another thing. This was Chloe Hummel, after all, with her pink toenails in his hands.

"You wanna hear a great idea?" Chloe said suddenly.

"Sure," Jesse said.

"Let's slide around in the snow on the terrace."

"Absolutely great," Jesse said, having been prepared for anything she might have suggested.

Up she got, Chloe Hummel did, and went over to the terrace door, glass in hand.

"My God, what a storm," she said, looking out at the swirl of it, the depth of it.

"I told Marion last night that it wasn't going to be—"

"I remember," Chloe said.

"Aren't you going to be cold in just that thing?"

"Colder than that," Chloe said, swooping the nightie up and over her head, creating voluminous, stunning nudity.

"Come on," she said, "take your clothes off."

Jesse followed her obediently.

By the time he was undressed Chloe had unlatched the terrace door and was outside.

The cold prevented Jesse's body from displaying passion.

He ran toward her down the terrace and collided with her, slipping down into the snow, tangled up with her.

"Shit, man, shit, man," Chloe said, delighted, trembling.

"Shit, man, shit, man," Jesse repeated, picking her up, fighting the wind, carrying her back inside, dumping her on the living room floor at his feet.

"Shower shower, fast fast," Chloe said, laughing.

They showered in Norman's bathroom, plugging the drain, sliding down into the warm water, letting the shower go on and on.

They called Marion from Jesse's own phone, lying in Jesse's own bed.

"Honey, what in the world happened?" Chloe asked her sister.

"I was asleep, and then pow! I never felt such pain in my life," Marion said.

"Why didn't you wake me up?" Chloe asked, on her back with Jesse's head on her breast.

"I knew that Jesse would know where to go. I mean, it's his neighborhood."

"He said you had to walk."

"It was the biggest nightmare of my life," Marion said. "He really came through. Did he go to school?"

"I suppose so, I haven't seen him," Chloe said.

"I'll find him later on the phone. And listen, don't come over here until it stops snowing. It's a real hike, believe me."

"Are you in a private room?" Chloe asked, holding the receiver in the crook of her neck, reaching for her champagne glass on the night table.

"It's a semiprivate. It'll do," Marion said.

"Did the operation hurt?" Chloe asked. She ran her left hand through Jesse's hair.

"Who knows, I was out of it. I have some pain now, but oh, Chloe, you should never have to live through what I lived through last night. Thank God for Jesse."

"That's great," Chloe said.

"Sweetie," Marion said, in a somewhat softer voice, "would you stay there and just look after Jesse until I get back?"

"Of course," Chloe said.

"They say ten days, or something like that. Is it an imposition?"

"Not in the least. I'll make plans. I was going to L.A., but I'll go later."

Jesse, catching the drift of it, gave Chloe a silent kiss on the cheek.

"Anything you need?" Chloe asked.

"My makeup bag, my toothbrush, panties, stuff like that. I'll tell Jesse later, or something," Marion said. "Listen, a nurse has just come in, I gotta go."

"We'll be fine over here," Chloe said.

"We *are* fine over here," Jesse said, after Chloe hung up.

"Now hear this, little man, you know what 'prolong' means?"

"Please don't insult me," Jesse said.

"Well, this is a good time for that particular word. I realize we were in the tub and all, but *this* is a good time for it, don't you think? A good opportunity?"

Chloe slid her index finger under his chin, and held his face up to hers.

"Yes," Jesse said meekly, "it is."

"Seize it," Chloe said.

"HOW MUCH MONEY do you have," Chloe asked him.

"You mean my father?"

"No, you."

They were still in Jesse's bed, having taken a nap, having found another bottle of champagne, having chilled it in the freezer.

"I have a checking account," Jesse said.

"How much."

"About fifteen hundred dollars."

"I wanted to go out and get us some food," Chloe said. "Make us a feast."

"You can just charge everything at the market. I'll call them. Or I could come with you."

"No, I want to surprise you."

Chloe got out of bed and stood by the window.

"Shit, man, it's never gonna stop snowing," she said, her body caught in the white light of winter.

"Is there any more champagne?" Jesse asked.

"Half a bottle. Plenty," she said. "And there's a bottle of red wine for lunch."

Chloe jumped on him, her breasts all over his face, and kisses galore. "Hmm," she said, "you're my Nellie Fox."

"Why him?" Jesse asked, hoping for the best.

"He's not really graceful, like, say, Jerry Coleman, or Gil McDougald, but he gets the job done."

"Like Eddie Stanky?"

"Poo," Chloe said, lying on Jesse from top to bottom. "Who'd fuck Stanky. Not me, little man."

CLANKING IN THE kitchen. What a commotion!

Jesse lay in bed, listening to the radio. The second movement of Mozart's Twenty-ninth Symphony. Lying on his side, he closed his eyes, his ear right up to the speaker. "I am so happy," he said in a whisper.

Chloe, in her terry-cloth robe, brought him another glass of champagne.

"What have we here, a true music lover?" she said, sitting at his feet, the way Marion often did while saying good night.

"Norman Savitt's son, you know," Jesse said.

"There was a time when I wanted to be a singer," Chloe said. "But I'm not talented that way. My singing is kind of like a dull noise."

"Who do you like?" Jesse asked, shoving two pillows under his head, and turning to lie on his back under the covers.

"Come on now, Billie Holiday. And I like Ella Fitzgerald."

"Would you sing something for me later, if I played the piano for you?"

"I don't mind, but don't expect much. I'm an actress, that's all."

"But that's a lot," Jesse said, encouraging her by raising his eyebrows.

"You want to know the truth?" Chloe said, drawing her knees up and surrounding them with her arms. "Acting is just being yourself, only just a little different. It's instinctive. I don't believe all this crap about sense memories, and all that Actors Studio stuff. You *are* who you *are.* I know all about Brando, and all that stuff, but it seems to me so pretentious, you know what I mean? I'd never tell Marion this. And we're really not all that close, if the truth be known. We see things differently. She thinks Lee Strasberg is some kind of God. All that preparation for two lines, or something. It's ridiculous. That's what Marion did all the time. She over-everythinged. It's ridiculous, it really is. Jimmy Stewart is Jimmy Stewart, and there's no better actor in the world."

"I don't know much about it," Jesse said, "but Marion and her friends really work at it. They rehearse here sometimes, so I know."

"You know what it's like?" Chloe said. "It's like trying to be in *control* of yourself all the time. Everything so rehearsed, based on some kind of supposed motivation. Shit on motivation. I did a play once, in which I played a butterfly. I promise, a butterfly. Marion would have gone back into the cocoon—is that it?—'to find the moth within me.' Screw the moth. The moth doesn't count. It's the butterfly that's in the play. I was cast because I was somebody's idea of a butterfly. It wasn't a William Inge play, you know. It was a light little piece. And somebody's asking me to find the moth within me? Shit, man, what a waste of time. That's why Marion and me will never know each other too well, you know?"

"Maybe you're right," Jesse said almost gravely.

"You're goin' to love dinner, I'm tellin' you," Chloe said. "I'm a little drunk."

"You want any help in the kitchen?" Jesse asked.

"None. It's the element of surprise. I'll be ready in twenty minutes, tops."

"Hey, Chloe," Jesse said.

"What," she said.

"You're the best," Jesse said.

"And you haven't even eaten," Chloe said.

THEY SAT AT Norman's dining room table eating Chloe's feast: leg of lamb with roasted everything—potatoes, carrots, and squash touched with cinnamon.

"This is the single best meal of my entire life," Jesse said.

"It's easy," Chloe said. "It just comes natural. Some girls know, some girls don't. You know, I'm tipsy, but good tipsy," she said, sitting on one leg, leaning way over her plate.

"Would you say you're drunk?" Jesse asked.

"Shit no," Chloe said. "I can drink anyone under the table. Poo, I just had a little wine. Tipsy wine, I call it."

Chloe's natural hunger for everything, her (to Jesse) exclusive talents, were greater in one single person than he had ever imagined possible. White Sox talk, cinnamon squash, my God.

"I have fallen in love with you," Jesse announced quite suddenly.

"That's terrific," Chloe said with a mouthful of lamb.

"How long can you stay with me," Jesse asked, having stopped eating after his declaration, very serious now with his plan-making.

"I'm supposed to go to California, but I don't have any money," Chloe said.

"Why California?"

"There's a big audition in L.A., but I wrote it off because I can't get there."

"I'll get you there," Jesse said, searching her eyes dramatically.

"How are you going to get me there," Chloe said.

"I have an account."

"You said fifteen hundred dollars."

"I think there's more. I know there's more."

"I couldn't take your money," Chloe said.

"I'll lend it to you," Jesse said, devoted to the project.

"But I've got to cover for Marion. I mean, I can't leave you here alone."

"I'll come with you," Jesse said.

"You say you'll come *with* me?"

"That's what I said. I'll just fly out with you. Maybe I'll see my father, then I'll fly back. But at least we could have the time together. How long would you have to stay?"

"I don't know. Maybe a long time. It would depend."

"What are your true feelings about this?" Jesse asked.

"About Marion?" Chloe said.

"I'll be back before she's out of the hospital," Jesse said, determined.

"She's gotta know, though," Chloe said.

"I'll tell her. She doesn't run my life."

Jesse got up and paced around the table

"I've gotta trust you, I guess," Chloe said.

"That's what you've gotta do," Jesse said, stopping to point a finger at her. "You've got to really trust me."

CHLOE TOLD MARION about a big audition in Los Angeles. "Jesse wants to come along to see his father. To surprise him. Should we let him?"

Jesse, on the extension phone, promised Marion that he'd

be back within three days, in plenty of time to help her home from the hospital.

"Isn't this a little bizarre?" Marion asked them both, her voice a bit weak.

"Why bizarre?" Jesse asked, feeling no heat from Marion, aware that he would travel across the country unopposed.

"I don't know," Marion said.

"Everything's on the up and up," Chloe said.

"I don't know if this is irresponsible, or what it is," Marion said, suddenly sounding to Jesse as if she were digging in for debate.

"Don't be ridiculous," he said, feeling impatient, put upon.

"You don't have to shout," Marion said.

"Did I shout? Chloe, did I shout?" Jesse asked, standing at his father's desk.

"I didn't hear you shout," Chloe said, on the up and up, "but you've got to understand, Marion's had an operation."

"You guys, I don't know," Marion said, with a little laugh that relinquished her claim on them.

"Well then," Chloe said, in a tone that Jesse heard as eagerness.

"And I'll call you from every step of the way," Jesse said to Marion. "What can I get for you?" he added, slowing it down just a little, exhibiting, he felt, a casual gait: nothing unusual here; if you want me to come over with some toiletry, why, golly, of course, of course.

"I'm OK," Marion said, the little laugh gone.

"This audition is a big chance for me, or else I wouldn't be going," Chloe said.

"I can understand," Marion said.

———

JESSE PAID FOR everything: the taxi to Idlewild, hot dogs at the airport, wine on the plane, sandwiches at the Chicago airport, a Chicago White Sox coffee cup at the Chicago airport—a present for Chloe.

And the taxi from the Los Angeles airport to an apartment on Franklin Avenue that belonged to a friend of Chloe's, an actor named Charley, "some guy from Chicago," Chloe had said on the plane.

"Are we near Cañon Drive?" Jesse asked the driver, feeling his father's presence.

"Do you want me to take it?" the driver asked.

"Is it out of the way?" Chloe asked, peculiarly impatient.

"It's one way to where you're going," the driver said.

"Can we drive down it?" Jesse asked. "Where's 632 Cañon?"

"It's on the way."

In a while they passed Norman's house.

It was one o'clock on a warm Wednesday afternoon. To Jesse, his father's place, splashed by sunshine, looked like some kind of spacious Spanish villa. He kept this observation to himself, feeling that it was ridiculous, a Spanish house in Beverly Hills, California. He realized that he had no sense of architecture, that he had absorbed little information about the world, that he was ignorant, stubborn, and pontifical on the tiny little subjects he had been able to grasp. Chloe's worldliness had opened his eyes. He would have to learn and learn and learn in order to keep up with her.

"Nice," Chloe said, about 632 North Cañon Drive, as they drove by.

Jesse felt his father disappear behind him. Without moving his lips, without making a sound, he said to himself: I'm a jerk.

THERE WAS A key under the doormat that Chloe knew all about.

A bedroom, a living room, and a kitchenette.

Green shag carpeting, pink linoleum in the kitchenette, ornately framed watercolors of lakes and mountains in every room. Huge electric fans in the bedroom and living room turned to HIGH, clattering noisily. Two books about chess on the living room coffee table—the only two volumes Jesse could spot.

An apartment in general disarray: clothes thrown everywhere, cowboy boots in the middle of the unmade bed, movie magazines piled in corners—dozens of them. A couple of black-and-white photos of Chloe mixed in with a handful of playing cards on the living room floor: Chloe on a street corner in a bonnet, just standing there in a winter coat, looking bulky and coy.

"Isn't this a cute little place?" Chloe said, throwing her bag on the bed.

"Have you ever been here before?" Jesse asked.

"Oh sure, I live here sometimes," Chloe said, unzipping her bag.

"I didn't realize that," Jesse said, not knowing whether to sit down, or exactly what.

"I pay Charley some rent whenever I can," Chloe said, taking two aspirin, swallowing without water. "Jesus, do I have some kind of headache."

"Where will I stay?" Jesse said, standing in the foyer.

"Right here," Chloe said, back in the living room, pointing to the couch.

"And you sleep with Charley?"

"Of course, dummy," Chloe said, laughing a little. "He's harmless."

"You said he was—what did you say he was?"

"He's bisexual, if that's what you mean," Chloe said, now

in the kitchenette, opening the refrigerator to look around.

"I see," Jesse said, not knowing what bisexual meant, feeling trapped, and embarrassed.

"Charley's made chocolate pudding!" Chloe said.

"Are you lovers?" Jesse asked softly.

"Aren't we all?" Chloe replied.

Then she did something unexpected. She came into the living room with a big red bowl in her arms, and, facing Jesse, who was still standing in the foyer, winked at him, a full-blown cataclysmic wink, so devoid of generosity, so remarkable for what it admitted, so entirely vulgar and irrevocable, that it sank Jesse to his haunches under a watercolor landscape in a silver-coated frame.

"Are you OK?" Chloe asked.

Jesse took a minute before he replied.

When he did, he addressed the floor. "I think I better go home," he said.

"Well, OK," Chloe said, dipping her middle finger into the chocolate pudding. "If that's what you want to do."

"Jesus," Jesse whispered to himself, but the noisy fans drowned him out.

"Don't you want to meet Charley?" Chloe asked, sitting down on the couch with the bowl in her arms.

"No," Jesse said.

"Look," Chloe said, with what Jesse took to be irritation, "I'm sorry."

"Chloe," Jesse said, using her name for the last time in her company, "you have nothing in the world to be sorry about. Believe me."

JESSE PHONED HIS father from the Los Angeles airport, charging the call to his own New York number.

"Where are you?" Norman said.

"At Ninety-sixth and Broadway," Jesse said, trying to account for the background noise.

"Is everything OK?" Norman asked.

"I just wanted to say hello. Actually, I'm in the subway."

"You sound like you're next door," Norman said. "How's Marion doing?"

"She's making progress," Jesse said, his eyes filling with tears.

"You've handled the whole thing wonderfully, Jesse boy."

"Daddy," Jesse said.

"I can hardly hear you suddenly."

"What's the date you're coming home?"

"It's sometime in late April. Around the twentieth. I'm writing an absolutely marvelous score."

"How many songs?" Jesse asked.

"Seven or eight. But God knows how many there'll be when all is said and done. I've got a *great* new ballad. I'm right at the piano, would you like to hear it?"

"Of course," Jesse said, turning his back to the airport, facing the inside of the phone booth.

"No lyrics yet, just the melody."

And Jesse listened to his father play.

A flight was announced. Jesse put his hand over the phone to prevent Norman from hearing it.

Halfway into the song, Jesse held the receiver away from his ear for a moment so that he could wipe his eyes with the palm of his right hand. He found that his cheeks were covered with tears. He used his sleeve as best he could.

From the receiver a foot or so away, he could hear his father playing. He had written a ballad in a minor key, a little tinny sound from a distance, calling to Jesse from home.

CRAZY

Jesse discarded an ace of clubs thinking it was the ace of spades, which he also held.

"It was a mistake," he said, most seriously. "Let's play the hand again."

"What?"

"It was just a mistake, that's all. Let's play it again."

"What do you *mean*, play it again. Are you *crazy*?"

ON SEVENTY-NINTH AND Columbus, waiting for a bus, Jesse said to an old woman who was also waiting for the bus: "Dancing could really do you a lot of good. It could revive you. Even in 1967 there are still Arthur Murray places. It's not too late. I mean it. You could—"

"Assault!" the old woman yelled.

"What do you mean *assault*?" Jesse yelled back.

A clerk in a store behind them heard the woman's cry and called 911. In about a minute, after Jesse and the woman had subsided, a police car materialized.

"Assault!" the woman suddenly resumed.

"Did he hurt you, lady," a cop asked, moving toward Jesse.

"I didn't touch her," Jesse said. *"Ask* her."

"Did he touch your person," the cop asked the woman.

"No, but he was obscene," the woman said.

"I wasn't obscene," Jesse said with disgust. "My name is Jesse Savitt," he said, handing his wallet to the cop, now fortified by another.

"I made a remark. I suggested that she learn to dance. That's the extent of it."

"Goon," the second cop said.

"I can't challenge that," Jesse said. He took money out of his pocket. "Please accept this ten-dollar bill and take a cab," Jesse said to the woman.

"You wanna press charges," one of the cops asked the woman.

"There's a cab," Jesse said, hailing it.

He helped the woman into it.

Through the open window, the woman said to him: "You're not playing with a full deck."

Jesse thought this remark was incongruous and appealing.

"You think it's funny?" one of the cops asked Jesse.

"Do I think *what's* funny," Jesse said.

"You guys think you're fuckin' hotshots."

"I don't. *Clearly* I don't," Jesse said.

JESSE BOUGHT THE rope at a hardware store with what little money he had left. He went to Fifty-seventh and Fifth and approached a man on the southwest corner.

"I'm with the city," he said. "We're taking a measurement survey. Would you be good enough to hold on to this end of the rope."

"Fine," the man said cheerfully.

Jesse crossed Fifty-seventh Street with the rope, holding his hand up to traffic.

On the northwest corner he found a construction worker on a break, eating a hot dog.

"I'm with the city," Jesse said. "We're taking a measurement survey. "Would you be good enough to hold on to *this* end of the rope while that guy over there holds on to *his* end of the rope."

"But the cars and crap."

"We have a permit," Jesse said.

"You're authorized."

"Officially."

"I'll hold it here," the man said, holding the hot dog in his left hand, accepting the rope with his right hand.

Jesse walked west on Fifty-seventh Street.

From a distance he turned to watch.

He heard much horn-blowing. The two men held the rope.

Jesse walked farther west, then turned again.

Traffic was blocked at Fifth and Fifty-seventh. The men held their ground.

The men held their ground for nearly ten minutes.

Policemen arrived.

Jesse crossed Sixth Avenue, walked up toward Seventh, and ducked into the BMT subway.

While waiting for the train he thought he had pulled off a pretty good practical joke. If caught, he'd be jailed. His father, a decent man, would be summoned. They would meet, bars between them, in a grim environment. "Daddy, I'm losing control," Jesse imagined himself saying, into the injured eyes of Norman Savitt. "Why?" Norman would ask, bewildered. "It was an act of aggression, and a not very amusing one," Jesse would say. Norman would lower his head, as he did in crises.

On the subway, Jesse lowered his head the way his father often did.

He got off the train at Forty-second Street, and drifted into a porno shop.

"I'm looking for the collected works of W. H. Auden," he said. "The great poet."

"You talkin' 'bout poems?" the clerk said.

"I most certainly am," Jesse said.

"You all wrong in here," the clerk said.

"Very well," Jesse said.

He felt dizzy on the street. Although the afternoon was clear and cool, unusually so for just before Labor Day, Jesse felt stifled by the heat. He found he was perspiring.

In a bar he had two shots of Scotch and a chaser of Piel's beer, the least expensive. His total worth was down to three hundred dollars, with no reliable income in sight.

Jesse went into the filthy men's room to look at himself in the mirror, thinking he had developed a rash on his forehead.

There was no mirror in the men's room—only a toilet without a seat, and a sink with no running water.

Jesse sat down on the side of the toilet bowl, and remained there for a half hour. During that time no one came into the men's room. Jesse would have said, was prepared to say, "Please forgive me, the room is in use," but it turned out it wasn't necessary.

SOON AFTER HE got home, the phone rang.

Jessica Morelli was calling for the first time in almost two years. She was calling after receiving nearly twenty letters from Jesse. Many of the letters had run well past thirty typewritten pages. Through it all, Jessica had maintained her silence, having parted with Jesse, having left him, having moved to Venice, California, at age thirty-eight. Jesse, twenty-nine, had never thought of those nine years as unusual. Jessica Morelli knew sexual tricks, unacrobatic but remarkable in retrospect. Jesse called her "a professional sensualist." In his mind, this professional sensualist had met her match in his small apartment on 100th Street near Riverside Drive. For over a year they had kept it up; Jessica down from Boston and new in town, living in a sublet with her daughter, Sharon, teaching the Alexander massage technique, and depending on Jesse and his jagged day-to-day of it. His friends were writers and actors, *involved* with New York. And Jesse, drinking and wild and funny and so many years younger, commandeering a divorced woman with an eight-year-old child with whom she shared a double bed in a new SoHo high rise. She would make the long subway journey into Jesse's tumultuous life, into his wonderful jazz music, into his bed, into his arms, knowing, but not revealing to him, that she would leave him someday soon, leave his volcanic youth. "I'm not in your element," she would say now and then, but Jesse didn't hear her. Jesse bathed her. Jesse took photographs of her. Jesse praised her very good looks.

Jessica Morelli hated New York. Like Boston, the climate was hostile; her extremities froze so easily, even in November and in March. And her former husband, only two hundred and fifty miles north, longed for her return, whining on the phone, pleading in his letters: *"We were married fifteen years."*

Jesse, a beginning journalist, sent everything he wrote to Venice, California. He composed short stories for Sharon, who had once said, "You're the best friend I can ever *hope* to have." He wrote sexual essays and mailed them to Jessica's heart. His once-a-month cleaning lady had said: "The wall behind your pillow is black with dirt." "Those are my dreams," Jesse had said, and then he told Jessica in a letter about the black wall and his dreams.

Nothing had pried her loose. Venice, California, had gobbled her up. Probably she was in love: so much youth out there, so many drugs, so much sun, so much Jefferson Airplane. Jesse, with his Miles Davis on 100th Street, didn't stand a chance.

Jessica was coming to town, could she stay with Jesse over the Labor Day weekend?

"Why are you coming to New York?"

"To sign some papers about taxes, and to see a publisher."

"What do you mean, a publisher."

"I want to write a book about what real enlightenment can mean."

"Enlightenment?"

"I think you'll understand when I tell you."

"Tell me now."

"No."

"That's all right. Tell me when you get here."

"I hope you're well."

"I'm fine, just fine. Working away. Things are good."

"Jesse?"

"Yes?"

"I'm coming under one condition."

"Yes?"

"That you forget about miracles."

"Jessica, sweetheart, please *believe* me. It never entered my mind."

JESSE HAD FORTY-EIGHT hours to work with. There was much to do: rugs cleaned, flowers purchased and arranged, refrigerator stocked—fruit and ice cream and enormous steaks and Nova from Zabar's and lobster meat from the Citarella fish market and William Greenberg brownies.

Jesse hired two Columbia students to clean the apartment top to bottom for fifty dollars each.

Jesse bought four throw pillows for the living room couch.

Jesse spent all but thirty of his three hundred dollars, and charged well over two hundred dollars.

Jesse told friends on the phone about Jessica's visit.

"It's more of a return, really," he said. "She's drawn here to me in some way. I can't begin to understand it, but the passion is there."

Jesse wanted to weigh 180 at Jessica's arrival. He fasted on Thursday, ignoring the lobster and Nova and brownies.

He weighed himself on Friday morning and found a 179. Continuing his fast until noon, he weighed himself once an hour, finishing at 178 ½.

Jesse decided that during Jessica's stay he wouldn't weigh himself. But if the scale was there, how could he prevent the inevitable?

He called Brian, the man who lived next door on the seventh floor. He asked Brian if he would accept a bathroom scale, just for the weekend. Brian laughed, and said he would accept Jesse's scale, that he would slide it under his living room couch and return it to Jesse on Tuesday.

Jesse took the scale over to Brian's apartment.

115

Brian was a high school teacher, a single man who frequently traveled with other single men to the Orient. Brian Millhouse. Jesse was always reassured when Brian Millhouse came back from the Orient at the end of August. Four summers had gone by, during which Brian had followed this routine. Now he was back, and ready to accept Jesse's scale.

"It's eccentric, I'll admit," Jesse said, in Brian's living room.

"I can understand," Brian said, with unsatirical assurance.

"I mean, I weigh one seventy-four, and I don't want to *deal* with it over the holiday. I'm so disciplined with this scale, sometimes it drives me crazy."

"I have my quirks, too."

He was a short man about forty years old. For a moment Jesse imagined that Brian's main quirk was an ongoing attempt to make himself taller by the use of a stretching apparatus in someone else's apartment. Brian would tie himself into or onto the machine, and activate a device that would pull at his limbs and his hair and his bones, so that, in time, with repeated visits to the friend's apartment, Brian would begin to grow taller. Perhaps the process would add two or three inches. In time.

"What are your quirks?" Jesse asked.

"I'm meticulous about my teeth," Brian said.

"What do you mean?"

"I mean, I brush my teeth four times a day, no matter where I am in the world."

"That doesn't sound so quirky," Jesse said, disappointed. "It sounds to me like good hygiene."

"Well, there are some people who think I overdo it. So I can understand your scale thing."

Jesse's friend Maxine called him early in the afternoon.

"Honey," she said, "would you take Tara for me until Tuesday? I'm going upstate."

"I can't," Jesse said.

"Why?" Maxine asked.

"I can't have a cat in the house."

"But when I've been there, Tara's been with us. She sleeps in the *bed* with us. I don't—"

"I'll *take* your fuckin' cat. How's *that*," Jesse said.

"Honey, what's the matter?" Maxine asked.

"Nothing," Jesse said.

"I think you just resent my call, my asking a favor. You've got to keep in mind that all I do for you are favors. I get your laundry done, I pick up stuff in the Village for you. I mean, I run errands. This is just *Tara.* You know?"

Jesse spoke slowly. "I said, I'll take your cat."

"You said 'fucking cat.'"

"I didn't mean it."

"You've got to learn to be more civil," Maxine said.

"Don't civil me," Jesse said. "Bring the cat before three-thirty."

"All right, but don't be—"

"I'm not *being.*"

After Maxine's call, Jesse began to think that Tara could be used to his advantage. Tara would show Jessica the family side of Jesse, the unlikeliest man in town to care for an animal. *Jesse had changed. Jesse is more mature. He has a cat, his house is in order. He can afford caviar and Nova.*

Maxine came at three. She was a tall girl with long blond hair and narrow green eyes. She was most apologetic about Tara. The invitation came at the last minute, it was the last time she could get out of town until Christmas, would Jesse forgive her for calling at the last minute?

Of course Jesse would forgive her. Jesse loved Tara. Jesse was just in a bad mood earlier. You're lookin' sexy, Max.

Maxine submitted herself to Jesse in the front hallway, standing, somewhat undressed, Tara circling her ankles.

"Where upstate?" Jesse asked as they buttoned and buck-led.

"Ellenville," Maxine said.

"I don't know Ellenville," Jesse said.

"My sweet Tara," Maxine said, holding the cat, kissing the cat's face. "Have a good weekend, Tara-bara."

An hour before Jessica's scheduled arrival, it became important to Jesse to know his weight at the point in time of Jessica's return. "I was one seventy-nine that evening," he would say in the future, recounting the story of the week-end.

He phoned Brian, but got no answer.

He knocked on Brian's door. There was no reply.

He went downstairs to the lobby and rang Brian's buzzer. No one rang back.

Jesse went out into the street and looked up at Brian's seventh-floor living room window. It was open, ever so slightly. Jesse could shove it wide, hop into the apartment, take off his clothes, weigh himself, put the scale back under the couch. He would go upstairs, unlock his own front door, and then come down again. A simple trip up the fire escape, and then back into his own place. There was plenty of time, no rush.

On the third floor, Jesse stumbled on a solitary brick placed in front of a plant. The brick slipped away and fell to the street, narrowly missing a woman wearing a black hat and veil. She burst into a trot as the brick slammed onto the sidewalk a foot or so to her right.

"I'm so sorry!" Jesse yelled down. "No harm done!"

The woman really had some speed going, and paid no attention to Jesse.

By the seventh floor, Jesse was breathing heavily and perspiring freely. He thought that the physical activity might shave half a pound or so off his weight. He knew he'd need a quick shower before greeting Jessica.

To Jesse's surprise, an enormous crucifix lay over Brian's living room couch.

"Holy Jesus," Jesse said, astonished.

He pulled the scale out from under the couch and undressed completely, throwing his clothes over the crucifix.

As he was about to weigh himself he realized that Brian's plush green carpeting would distort the Detecto scale. Jesse stepped into the linoleumed hallway and onto the scale. The light was dim, making it difficult to see the dial.

Jesse studied the numbers gravely. It looked to him as though he had gained two pounds during this one Friday; that his fast had been meaningless; that his tomato juice and chicken noodle soup had ganged up on him. Maybe the salt had contributed to water retention.

He heard the front door open; no fumbling with the keys. Obviously someone familiar with the lock.

In a moment, Jesse, naked on his scale, faced a stranger, a man resembling Brian but with a full head of red hair, a plaid scarf around his neck. The man had entered the apartment briskly, had slammed the door, had locked the inside lock, and had come down the hall to discover Jesse around the bend. He let out a moan of fright that quickly built into a sirenlike wail.

"I'm the neighbor," Jesse said, remaining on the scale. "I'm a friend of Brian's. I'm weighing my options."

The siren wail turned to tears. The man crushed the scarf to his face.

"I live *next door*," Jesse said.

There were great intakes of breath, and sobbing, from the man with red hair.

119

"Let me help you," Jesse said, getting off the scale, moving toward the man.

"God oh God oh God," the man shrieked, darting past Jesse in the narrow hallway.

Jesse picked up the scale.

"When you tell Brian, tell him it was just *Jesse*. His pal Jesse. Got it?"

The wailing, now in the living room, was intense.

Jesse, leaving his clothes, ran to the front door, holding the scale under his arm.

He fumbled with the lock. It took a while to disengage himself from Brian's apartment. During that time, the weeping in the living room grew even louder.

Jesse raced out onto the seventh-floor landing.

The elevator door opened as Jesse raced by, heading for his own unlocked door.

He stumbled.

The scale slipped from beneath his arm, and shot away from him as if it were lubricated, landing with a grating crash on the emerging right foot of Jessica Morelli.

JESSE TOOK JESSICA to the St. Luke's emergency room. Jessica's foot was X-rayed. It turned out she had suffered a bad bruise.

Jessica had been a stoic in the cab, and while waiting for the X-ray. She had listened to Jesse's explanation unjudgmentally.

Jesse had told her that just before he got in the shower his doorbell rang and when he opened his door, no one was there, and because no one was there or on the landing, he wandered out for just a second to make sure that everything was OK, and it was then that Brian Millhouse, his neighbor, appeared with Jesse's scale, returning it to Jesse after borrowing it for a visiting friend for the week. Apparently, it seems that Brian's phone rang just as he knocked on Jesse's door, and he returned to his own apartment to answer it, and then, coming back with the scale, encountered Jesse on the landing, had handed him the scale, quickly scampered back into his apartment, embarrassed by Jesse's condition. Then Jessica came out of the elevator, and, "I mean it, Jessica, can you *believe* it, a *million*-to-one shot, the whole thing."

Back in Jesse's apartment, Jessica sank into the couch, and onto Jesse's new throw pillows. She elevated her foot on one arm of the couch, and asked for a ginger ale.

"I have everything *but* ginger ale," Jesse said.

"Just some water would be fine," Jessica said.

"No drink?" Jesse asked.

"I don't use any stimulants anymore," Jessica said, closing her eyes.

Jesse took a quick look at her before going to the kitchen to get a glass of water. He thought she was a spectacular beauty, with her absolutely oval face and long dark brown hair and vivid cheekbones, so rare in a face so round; and her gifted body, an exaggeration of the idea. She was nearly forty years old, her head now filled with the wisdom of the West. She had sworn off drugs, raising a little girl on her own, probably accepting only modest child support from Boston; a quite exceptional woman from Brookline, once secretarial and tentative, eventually the wife of a dentist, a careful and amusing mother, Sharon's best friend, except for Jesse, and *with* Jesse a professional sensualist.

"Since when have you had a cat?" Jessica asked, accepting a glass of water while spotting Tara for the first time, asleep on a chair across from her.

"About a year," Jesse said. "She's really no problem at all."

"I thought you hated cats," Jessica said, reclining again.

"I don't in fact. Tara's good company."

Jesse was pleased that Jessica remembered *anything* about him; his long letters had been sent, he imagined, to a black hole, to a woman who had wiped him off the face of the earth. But see? She remembered that he didn't like cats. *He was still alive.*

"Where'd you get it?" Jessica asked.

"I went to the ASPCA. I thought they'd have the gentlest animals."

"What's its name?"

"Tara."

"Why Tara?"

"There's a political analyst named James Tara I interviewed about next year's elections."

"Are you doing a lot of pieces?" Jessica asked, sipping her water.

"Actually, I'm working fairly regularly," Jesse said, sitting on the couch by her feet.

"You always wanted to write about news," Jessica said, smiling at him.

Jesse saw this as an invitation to hold her feet in his lap.

"Ow," Jessica said.

"Sorry," Jesse said.

"Would you rub my back?" Jessica asked.

"Of course," Jesse said. "Let's turn you over."

Jessica raised her torso, stripped off her T-shirt and bra, and carefully returned to the couch, face down, her arms above her head.

Jesse set to work, encouraged by the surprising sight of Jessica's naked breasts. He knelt on the floor beside her, working forcefully.

"Not too hard," Jessica murmured, her face turned away from him.

Jesse continued in silence, flirting with the side of her right breast.

"Your place looks nice," Jessica said, into the back of the couch.

"I've got a little money," Jesse said.

"It shows," Jessica said. "Hmm, right there, right there. The side of the spine."

Jesse leaned over and kissed Jessica's back. He took her lack of objection as permission.

"Hmm," she said.

"I think it's great you're going to write a book," he whispered into her spine.

"I've learned a lot," Jessica said.

"You mentioned enlightenment," Jesse said, expressing, he felt, spiritual advocacy. He had learned, almost entirely from women, the synthetic conduct of worship: his eyes moist with empathic interest, his voice a tender viola of appreciation. Often, such music brought on sex right then and there, at the beach, in a kitchen, clothes falling to the linoleum, or on the tennis court. *Take the ego away and you have truth.* How *right* they all were, these women. Most people aren't even *conscious,* for God's sake. Everything is so *changing.*

"It's about learning to live in a whole different way," Jessica said, turning to face Jesse.

"Do you mean in an enlightened way?" Jesse asked, feeding her her way.

"Enlightenment means being awake, and in a certain kind of harmony, and in direct touch with yourself. Being in complement."

"What do you mean?"

"Knowing your role in a group, and always being aware of the dynamics of that group. It is said that the opposite of talking is waiting. Being in complement means that there is no opposite to talking. Talking and waiting are all the same. Do you understand?" Jessica raised herself to her elbow.

"Of course I do," Jesse said. "I see it all around me. There's something in the air that's much different from anything I've ever known."

"It's that the eyes of the heart are always open," Jessica said, now resting on her side, the massage over.

"And that the heart is generous," Jesse added.

"There's a school of enlightenment on the West Coast called Luna. Have you heard of it?" Jessica asked.

"I haven't," Jesse confessed, lowering his eyes in disgrace.

"It's going to have an impact all over the world," Jessica said earnestly. "Its founder is a man from Brazil named Orlando, who is a genius. Luna is on the threshold of great domination. Oh Jesse, I'm being so simplistic. It's so much more than just domination. What it is, is a new *language,* a new space, a place that teaches you to *listen.*"

"Is that what you want to write about?" Jesse asked, lightly touching Jessica's breasts, to no response.

"I want to express what I feel. To write about Luna is to learn about Luna. That's what I want. To *learn.* When we met, when you and I met, I was, quite frankly, asleep. At least most of the time. I was a limited woman. I found myself in a satellite role to your planet, when we were together. Our communication was so *physical,* so wonderful in that way, but I realized that in most other ways I was just revolving around you in some kind of preordained period of time. A regular kind of thirty-eight-hour thing, around and around—a waitress, a secretary, always in some kind of subservient role, except when we were lovers, even though I'm nine years older. And the irony was, you were a baby, a slick baby in the big town. I don't want to get into this, really. You're a fine boy. I love your appetites."

Jessica sat up and put on her T-shirt. "Maybe I'll have a drink," she said.

"*Now* you're cookin'," Jesse said.

"ALL THAT FOOD," Jesse said after they'd eaten. "And yet look at you. You're almost a muscle woman."

"Lucky metabolism," Jessica said, leaning back in her kitchen chair.

"You have no jet lag, or anything?"

"It's easy coming East," Jessica said. "It's still early in my head."

"Nine o'clock for you, midnight for me."

Jessica got up, and limped into the living room, returning with her pocketbook. She took out a pack of cigarettes.

"Use the stove," Jesse said.

Jessica lit a cigarette with a burner. "See, I'm clean," she said with a laugh, returning to the table.

"You're conceptually sound anyway," Jesse said. He held out his hand to her, which she took.

He stood, and stepped forward to claim her. He bent over her. He kissed her. She responded to him, allowing her lips to part. His hand, once again, found her breast.

"Jesse," she said, as generously as she could, "I told you, no miracles."

"What do you mean," Jesse said, ahead of her, and distraught.

"Where's that old plaid quilt of yours," Jessica said.

"I don't know what you mean by miracle," Jesse said.

"Yes you do," Jessica said.

"You're going to sleep in the living room?"

"Me and Tara," Jessica said, touching his face with her hand.

"Let's negotiate," Jesse said, taking her hand and pulling her up.

"There are no issues to negotiate," Jessica said, walking behind him down the hall.

They sat facing each other on the couch, their legs crossed under them.

"I'll be forty in three months," Jessica said, dropping her cigarette in the nearly empty glass of water.

"Do you think that makes you ugly?" Jesse asked.

They had had several drinks while Jesse prepared dinner. Now, foggy from food and Scotch and desire, he heard his own strategy come tumbling transparently out of his cunning.

"No, I'm just telling you," Jessica said.

"Why are you telling me?" Jesse asked.

"Because I see your house is filled with good things for the kitchen table, and that you're taller in a certain sense. And that there's still nine years between us."

"I'd say that that actually *helped* us," Jesse said, without any particular plan.

"Then," Jessica said.

Neither of them spoke for a while.

"How's Sharon," Jesse finally asked.

"She's in art camp until after Labor Day, till next Tuesday. And she sends you her love. When I told her I was coming, she wanted to come with me."

"Why didn't she?" Jesse asked, following along, guilelessly.

"Because I didn't have the money," Jessica said with a warm smile.

"*I* could have sent it to you," Jesse said, touching Jessica's ankle.

126

"No matter. I mean, that's very nice." Jessica closed her eyes for a moment.

"Do you want to split a beer?" Jesse asked.

"I'd like a brandy," Jessica said. "I really haven't had a goddamn thing to drink in a year. This is good, if the truth be known." She rested her hand on Jesse's.

"Let's have brandy," Jesse said, getting up. "Remember our brandy nights?"

"Our brandy Sundays," Jessica said.

As he left the room a quick glimpse of her revealed to him the two years that had gone by. Jessica's two years: cross-country in a bus with an eight-year-old; the phone calls and letters from Boston, and from his very own typewriter, arriving constantly, simultaneously, documents imploring Jessica Morelli to return to the *home*, to New England dentistry, to Sunday brandies and subways from SoHo. Jessica scraping dollars together, finding accommodations, seeking out employment; Sharon waking in the dead of night, weeping from dreams, Jessica holding her child to her in some unfeasible rooming house, asleep and awake at the same time, her arms around her daughter, numbed by aloneness. Crow's-feet told of forty. Tiredness. Luna. Talking and waiting.

When Jesse returned with the brandies, Jessica's eyes were closed.

"Honey?" he said, putting the drinks on the coffee table.

Jessica was out, stuffed with his intentions.

Jesse got out the plaid quilt, and took a pillow from his bed. He set Jessica up, lifted her head, slid the pillow in, pulled her legs down so that she lay on the couch, kissed her bruised foot, turned out the lights, closed his own bedroom door, and lay down in the darkness of one in the morning, wide awake, close to tears.

NEAR DAWN, JESSE heard Jessica go down the hall to the bathroom. He heard her close the door. She ran the water in the sink, getting it cold, he knew from the past. A thirsty girl, detoxing from his brandy dance. Jesse thought of himself as poisonous, far from Luna, strictly a come-on kid, dangling drugs and odious mischief—not even mischief, too complimentary, that word. Dangling cruelty. This woman was out there on her own, fighting for her own life, for Sharon, trying to make something of it all. Returning to New York for a simple Labor Day stay, a week at most, she had had the poor luck to fall, with her radiant innocence still intact, into the quicksand of Jesse's jungle. He had her bruised and drunk in less than twelve hours. If she stayed long enough he would kill her.

Jesse sat up in bed to listen. He heard her turn the water off. He heard her flush the toilet.

He got out of bed and put on a robe. He opened his door when he heard the bathroom door open. He stepped into the hall into Jessica's arms. He crushed her to him. He tried to kiss her.

"No miracles, Jesse," she said.

"I can't take it," Jesse said.

"Sweetheart," Jessica said, disengaging herself from him.

"Will you at least just lie down with me?" Jesse asked, his voice filled with self-pity.

"Sleep, sweetheart," Jessica said, stepping around him, favoring her bruised foot.

"I can't," Jesse said.

A bit of light caught Jessica's nude body.

"You can," she said, facing him.

"Can I see you?" Jesse said.

"You're seeing me now," Jessica said.

"See you more?"

Jessica flipped on the hall light, and stood motionless, her arms at her sides.

"I'm going nuts," Jesse said, addressing everyone in the room. "I'm speaking from my heart."

Tara slithered into view, curling around Jessica's ankles.

"Because you can't have me?" Jessica said, picking Tara up and holding the cat to her bosom.

"This is just symptomatic," Jesse said, with, for the first time since her arrival, no tall tales to tell.

"Are you suggesting that the prince of sex can't get laid?" Jessica asked, with a surprising and sarcastic intensity.

"Laid is a metaphor," Jesse said.

"I'm not following you," Jessica said, backing away a little.

"Jessica, I can't get laid *anywhere.*"

"I can't help you," Jessica said coldly.

"What do you *mean,*" Jesse said, moving toward her.

"Go to sleep," Jessica said, turning, still holding the cat. Jesse followed her.

Near the couch he reached for her, but catching her off-balance, he pushed her.

Jessica fell, hitting her head on the corner of the glass coffee table.

Tara scampered away.

Jesse rushed to Jessica. He put his arms around her and pulled her to the couch and laid her down on her back.

There was enough light from the hall for Jesse to inspect the wound on her temple.

"I'm OK, I'm OK," she was saying.

She was bleeding, but quite conscious.

Jesse ran to the bathroom, grabbed a towel, and returned to Jessica.

He held the towel to her, wiping blood away.

"Shit," Jessica said.

"Please," Jesse said.

"Please nothing," Jessica said. "The quilt."

Jesse covered her.

"Get me a cold washcloth," Jessica said.

He did as he was told.

She took the cloth from him and held it to her head.

"Should we go back to St. Luke's?" Jesse said, with a piece of a smile.

"I'm getting out of here," Jessica said.

"Wait," Jesse said.

"I'll tell you this: if you write me one more fuckin' letter . . ." She closed her eyes dismissively.

"Do you think you had any part in it at all," Jesse said, standing, looking down at her.

Jessica didn't answer.

"Did you hear me," Jesse said.

"I heard you," Jessica said with her eyes closed.

"Well?"

"Get out of this room," Jessica said.

"This is my place," Jesse said.

"In a half hour you'll have it on your own."

"Do you think you had any part in it at all," Jesse said.

"I didn't do *nothin'* to you," Jessica said, her eyes popping open.

"Nor I to you, I don't think," Jesse said softly.

"You know what *I* think?" Jessica said. "You're a genetic error. How do you take to *that*?"

Jesse didn't answer for a while, and when he did, it was from the hall on the way to his room.

"I didn't know you had something like that in the shadows. I'll miss you less because of it, and more in spite of it.

I'm mortified. Tara's not my cat. Everything here is a prop.
Good-bye, Jessica."

"I can't be bothered," Jessica said.

"Yes," Jesse said.

Monday September 4, 1967

Dearest Dad,
Daddy:
I think the colon goes along better with the "Daddy." It kind
of toughens it up, takes away just the right amount of baby
fat. "Dearest Dad" and a colon is hypocritical, and even
belligerent, somehow, despite the "dearest." The "dearest"
in that case is just softening you up for the kill. I'm going
to hit you for money, or accuse you of wrongdoing toward
me, or the worst: confront you with your altogether stinko
performance in life, toward me, toward my mother when
she was alive, all of it untrue, so that the colon renders the
"dearest" sarcastic in the extreme. In other words, dearest
my foot. How about, Hey Pa. But the trouble is the period.
It makes the "Hey Pa" declarative, thus shutting off the flow
of subsequent information. The letter ends right there. Hey
Pa. Bye Pa. Hey Pa, you old son of a gun, how you doin'?
Bye Pa. Hey Pa with a comma is silly. It's the cheapest of
all possible worlds. "Pa," a word not known between us,
followed by a dimestore comma. If I were you I wouldn't
even read such a letter. Then there's the issue of Norman.
Calling you Norman is like eight-year-old boys who wear
hats; they're like grown-up guys making sales calls in the
late forties. Did Miller have Willie Loman in a hat? Would
that have been up to Kazan, or what? And "father" is not

even on our desk. It's like having breakfast in a cummer-bund. So I'm stuck with "Daddy," which has served me pretty well through all these years, and seems to get the best out of you. It keeps us both young, even in the face of evidence to the contrary. I won't burden you here with a new paragraph, knowing what I have to say. A new paragraph would be obscene in its calculation, in its attention to literature, in its narcissistic nod to the aesthetic of the page. I don't think I'm going to go on living much longer. I'm considering calling my life a day. I think that the basic catastrophe of life is that everyone has his own reasons. That's just general politics I'm talking about, the moment by moment of it, the rejection, romantic decisions, wisdom gone awry, sudden changes of the microscopic variety, just everything. For the fun of it I just looked up "politic." Listen to this: "Sagacious in promoting policy." That's precisely what I mean by the moment to moment of it. The policy of personal conduct, the sagacious promotion of the way one combs one's hair, the way one accepts an invitation, or clouds an issue, or drives a car, or holds a woman, or writes a letter. That's *policy* being sagaciously promoted. Now the word "sagacious" comes into play. Let me look it up. Listen to this: "Of keen and farsighted penetration and judgment." Also: "Caused by or indicating acute discernment." IN WHOSE OPINION? The policy holder's, of course. So to go back: the basic catastrophe—let me modify that, subdue it a bit—the basic *tragedy* of life is that everyone has his own reasons. HIS OWN POLICIES. What we're all busy doing is sitting back WITH OUR OWN POLICIES IN OUR POCK-ETS and at the same time judging the sagaciousness of the other guy's policies. And their promotion mechanisms. If they dance persuasively, if they come and sit at the lip of the stage and sing "Over the Rainbow," or dangle loot before our eyes if we'll only see it *their* way, so that we can then buy (or take) that loot and purchase food in order to subsist, or buy jewelry to give to a woman so that we can *promote sagaciously* our policy that clearly reads: *Sexual Intercourse* IS A GOOD THING *RIGHT NOW*—(and what is our private reaction to accepting the dangled loot? Do we think less of ourselves, or: do we give a damn-this-girl's-got-great-tits)? One's policy may be to earn the loot oneself, to enjoy "Over the Rainbow" simply as a gift of theater. One's policy may be to not even *think* the word "tit," but to think "breasts," or even more starch-collared yet: bosom. (Did you notice my policy about "bosom?" It was *me* who chose "starch-collared," rather than, say, "dignified," or even "appropriate," which is another policy altogether.) What I'm writing to you about, it now seems clear to me, is the death of a salesman. Me. I have run out of what little sagaciousness I ever had, I am totally ambivalent about practically all my policies, and my promotion department, ha! I'm trying to sell basketballs to midgets. Ha Ha! It's one of the rare cases of everything breaking down, so completely, so utterly completely, that there is very little sense in keeping the life support system working. Do I still find pleasure? How could I not. Music, artichokes, baseball, colors (especially light brown and rich orange), and I like the way beer looks in a glass, and the way Scotch whiskey looks in a Johnnie Walker Black Label bottle that's three-quarters full—more attractive than a full bottle: there's the implication of drink, the slight little toss of the Scotch if you move the bottle just a bit, the nice even cut of the liquor corresponding with the top of the label (or Label). And ownership, probably the most important Excellence of a three-quarters-full bottle. It is a property owned by you, an intimate property in your own house, long past the antiseptic purchasing point—the anonymity of the liquor store. It's strange, but bottles of Johnnie Black Label in Paris liquor stores are quite pleasing to me, but not in London, or here. I think it has to do with finding a friend where no English is spoken, and also—maybe—the romance of it, Paris and food and jazz music, and quite possibly sex, born from the bottle, and all that jazz. There's a family feeling to Paris liquor stores, too. Only Paris. As you know, I have no family history; after my mother died it was my Daddy and me living somewhere, and then another place, and schools, and long-distance calls from you, or from me to you, but no sense of family, unlike the French families who run the liquor stores into which one can peek from the street and view the dangerous bustle of intimacy. All of this, I think, is entirely dependent on one's relationship to booze. For the abstemious (from the *beginning* abstemious, I mean ten-year-olds growing up into forever—family policy, personal policy: "I tried it once and I didn't like the taste" is generally how they explain it), for these people there's no such interplay with liquor bottles. It might be Hershey bars, that dark brown wrapper, and candy stores, the same thing, only not with liquor (or it just might be simply: where we get our sugar). But it is the aesthetics of drinking that's a part of my pleasure. And the aesthetics of artichokes (have you ever seen them grow en masse? They sit like little hats on top of their plants, stretching as far as the eye can see). And the aesthetics of recordings—the vinyl, the packaging, the turntable itself, every bit as fine as the music dipped in lemon butter, mixing as I am for your reading enjoyment my pleasures on this planet. Beyond the pleasures just listed in this letter, there are others, many others, and if they all appeared here, my demise, as I contemplate it, would contradict the honor of my delights, and blur my place in our minuscule history, as a fragmented family, as friends, as father and son; and on my own, what little I've accomplished, published, spoken. My very integrity. And the remote prospect of your grandchildren. The perpetuation of our line. I would tarnish what I cherish. Am I beyond redemption? Will this letter find a mailbox? Is my purpose to alarm you, to elicit your sympathy, to shake loot from your tree by admitting my bankruptcy? To speak to you posthumously? To end my suffering, as I feel it, contemplate it? All of the above, I am utterly ashamed to admit. I have thirty-five Nembutals lined up on my desk, an army of little yellow killers. Could it be that I'm too lazy to take them? (Heaven knows, I'm lazy. When I'm asleep, I simply dream I'm sleeping. Ha Ha!) My dearest father, Norman Savitt, Pa, what awaits me now?

With love,
Jesse

Jesse took ten books with him, all but two of which were confiscated.

"No psychologically oriented literature," said an admissions officer, a bald Swede about forty who spoke gravely, economically.

"What's wrong with D. H. Lawrence," Jesse said, sitting on a straight-backed chair in a humorless office.

"You know as well as I do," the Swede said. His name was Malcolm Anderson. He wore a gray business suit and a gay yellow tie.

"I don't, honestly," Jesse said. "I can understand your position on *Tender Is the Night,* he went on, thinking he had bargaining power, "but really now, *Women In Love?* I don't get it. And Malcolm, please, just so I know. *Augie March?* And poems? Edna St. Vincent Millay, for Christ's sake?"

"You have come here, you'll adhere here," Malcolm said.

"I'll *adhere here?*" Jesse said, not really trying to keep derision from his laugh.

Malcolm Anderson allowed Jesse Savitt *The Magus* and *Lilith.*

Jesse's roommate was asleep on his back, a muscular man as bald as Malcolm. Their room faced the Henry Hudson Parkway. Though it was a sunny midday, the light was a February off-white that emphasized the unglamorous appointments: a rugged wooden desk, two matching armless chairs, and three black bureaus in a row along the far wall.

Jesse lay down on his bed and fell asleep immediately. He was awakened by a psychiatrist.

"Pardon me, Mr. Savitt."

Jesse opened his eyes.

"I'm Dr. Emerson."

"I want my books back," Jesse said.

"Let's talk about it," Dr. Emerson said. He was a young man with a cherubic face and a crew cut. He held a clipboard and a pen.

Jesse looked over to his roommate, who was gone.

"How are you?" Dr. Emerson said.

"I feel at a disadvantage, lying down," Jesse said.

"This is not an adversarial structure," Dr. Emerson said.

Jesse, swinging his legs over the side of the bed, sat up.

"Better?" Dr. Emerson said.

"Infinitely," Jesse said.

Dr. Emerson jotted something on the clipboard. Jesse could see that it was the word "infinitely." Then he noticed that Dr. Emerson was sitting on a folding metal chair that he had obviously brought into the room with him.

"Do you just carry that chair around?" Jesse asked.

"What is your interest in it," Dr. Emerson said.

"Do you just keep moving from one unadversarial structure to another?" Jesse said.

"Are you disturbed by that?" Dr. Emerson said.

"Give me a moment, and I'm fairly certain I'll become indifferent to it," Jesse said.

"Are you comfortable?" Dr. Emerson said.

"Conversationally or physically," Jesse said.

"Both," Dr. Emerson said.

"I'm off-balance, I'd say," Jesse said.

"In what sense of the word," Dr. Emerson said.

"Words," Jesse said. "I'm on foreign ground, and I'm unfamiliar with the currency."

"That's an interesting way of putting it," Dr. Emerson said.

"I'm flattered," Jesse said.

"You're furious," Dr. Emerson said.

"I'm fucked," Jesse said.

Dr. Emerson said nothing.

"Let's keep the *f*s going," Jesse said. "I'm fatigued."

He waited for Dr. Emerson, who remained quiet.

"I'm finished. And, interestingly, I'm famished. What's the eating structure," Jesse said.

"Supper is in the dining area at five-thirty," Dr. Emerson said.

"And drinks?" Jesse said. "Three-thirty or so?"

"Do you enjoy drinks?" Dr. Emerson said.

"I had a drink once, but I didn't like the taste," Jesse said.

"What kind of alcohol," Dr. Emerson said.

"I don't remember, it was so long ago."

"Really," Dr. Emerson said, jotting something down.

"You mean, five-thirty is dinnertime every night?" Jesse asked.

"That's it," Dr. Emerson said with a smile.

"Woe to the Spanish gent who winds up in here," Jesse said.

"Why is that?" Dr. Emerson said.

"Because in Spain, dinner is served at ten," Jesse said. "But I suppose that with dinner here at five-thirty, any kind of a ten-thirty meal, or snack, could be looked upon as breakfast, and the following morning's breakfast could be considered lunch, and so on and so on, until gradually we'd pick up time on Europe, decreasing the existing time difference, which I believe is five or six hours, until, at long last, there'd be *no* time difference between downtown Manhattan and downtown Madrid, and quite soon thereafter, we'd move ahead, which would upset the political balance of the globe, and at some point, with climate and other earthly circumstances accommodating this conceit—gravity, the whole concept of orbiting, things like that—at some point the galactic pressure would build to the bursting point, and there'd be a calamitous explosion, obviously catastrophic, that would result in millions of years of spacial realignment, a new planet capable of supporting life, or even *many* planets, for all we know, and the sophistication of the species over billions of years, the eventual emergence of language and history, and surely archaeology, which would lead to the discovery of orbiting artifacts from *our* period, and bit by bit, the understanding *by* this new species of the destruction of the previous administration, so to speak, and the eventual pinpointing of the cause of that destruction, imperceptible at first, even with all the data that would be available, but eventually it would all come into focus: *your* institution here in Riverdale, New York, and its structure of serving dinner at five-thirty."

Dr. Emerson jotted something down.

"I'll bet you're thinking: where to start," Jesse said.

Dr. Emerson said, "We've admitted you at the suggestion of Dr. Armstrong."

"*I* sought out Dr. Armstrong," Jesse said. "You've admitted me at my own suggestion."

"Do you regret it?"

"I wasn't prepared for the Spartanness. The ugliness," Jesse said.

"What do you find ugly?" Dr. Emerson asked.

"The lack of imagination."

"And how does that lack manifest itself?" Dr. Emerson said.

"In the life choices of you and your staff."

"How's that?" Dr. Emerson said, moving his chair back a little.

"How long have you been associated with this building?" Jesse asked.

"I'm not sure it's relevant," Dr. Emerson said.

"Don't you see, sir, our exchange can never transcend the level of your chair. And that makes me think I've made a mistake confiding in you."

"I don't follow your logic," Dr. Emerson said.

"Do you think you can be of help to me?" Jesse said.

"Only with your help," Dr. Emerson said.

"Do you feel that way about all of your patients?"

"Yes," Dr. Emerson said.

"I have a couple more questions," Jesse said.

"Shoot," Dr. Emerson said.

"Am I imprisoned here?"

"What do you mean."

"If I wanted to leave, could I?"

"No."

"What's to prevent me?"

"We have a fairly secure building," Dr. Emerson said.

139

"I have another question," Jesse said.

"Shoot," Dr. Emerson said.

"Is there a phone I can use?"

"Not for the first ten days."

"Why?"

"We wish you to experience the specifics of our program without the very things that got you into trouble in the first place."

"I understand," Jesse said.

"Anything else?" Dr. Emerson said.

"Do the men and women cohabit?"

"The women are in the south wing, the men in the north wing. You'll eat together. There can be no flirtation, or sexual turn of event. If you notice a problem of any kind along these lines, you *must* report the person or persons to me or Dr. Martinez, whom you'll meet, just as you yourself will be held accountable by the others currently in the building."

"Do you feel I'll go against your rules under the kind of scrutiny you've apparently developed?" Jesse asked.

"That's not for me to judge. Don't you agree?" Dr. Emerson said, rising.

"Of course it isn't," Jesse said.

Dr. Emerson folded his chair and picked it up.

"When do we talk again?" Jesse asked.

"We'll meet three times a week. This being Thursday, we'll meet Monday morning, right here. Fair enough?"

"What about the weekend?" Jesse asked, stung, suddenly, by claustrophobia.

"There's always help on the floor," Dr. Emerson said, moving to the door.

"Could I have my books back?" Jesse asked.

"I give you my word I'll look into it," Dr. Emerson said as he left.

"Dr. Emerson," Jesse said in something of a shout.

Dr. Emerson reappeared in the doorway, holding his folded chair.

"Wasn't this a short session?" Jesse asked.

"No," Dr. Emerson said.

"You realize, of course, that I'm not going to stay in this building long," Jesse said.

"Ah," Dr. Emerson said with a smile.

AT DINNER, JESSE sat next to a girl named Julie Sargent, a twenty-year-old with white skin, long light brown hair and embarrassed hazel eyes. She cast them down with each bite of her Del Monte fruit cup, and brought them back up into play for only seconds at a time.

"You should stay out of the sun," Jesse said.

"I seldom," Julie Sargent said.

"Do you have a roommate?" Jesse asked.

"No," Julie answered, dropping her eyes.

"Do you enjoy reading?" Jesse asked.

"That's her forte," Jesse's roommate said. He was sitting across a table of four, ignoring his meal.

The dining area, with five tables of the same size arranged in a circle, was wallpapered in plain light red. The linoleum floor was of a jarring and contradictory shade of green, an army hue with scuffs of brown—the years of solemn soldiers filing in and filing out had taken their toll. Though dusted and sponged, the room appeared unkempt, even soiled.

"She's got a ton of books," Jesse's roommate continued.

His name was Mark Olsen, and he had revealed to Jesse only moments before dinner that he was undergoing shock therapy. "I'm a nitwit," he had said, "so what harm can it do."

In fact, Jesse felt, Mark Olsen resembled a nitwit, without an Alfred E. Newman gleam of fun. Jesse had searched his eyes for little nitwit crosses, and had found, instead, limpid pools of absenteeism.

"How do you know she's got a ton of books?" Jesse asked.

"I was in there," Olsen said slyly. "She showed me her twat."

Julie Sargent's eyes closed. Tears leaked out, almost immediately abundant, attaching themselves to her eyelids, slipping down her face, leaping across space onto her hand and fork.

"Come on, Olsen," Jesse said, siding with Julie, "cut the shit."

"She showed me her twat," Olsen repeated, with greater fervor.

"Didn't," Julie said almost inaudibly.

"I know that," Jesse said. "It's nothing, Julie," he continued, putting his hand on her arm.

The fourth diner at the table, an aggressively thin woman about fifty, slammed her silverware to her plate, creating a clanking that threw everyone in the room into a sea of silence. The only lapping of the shore was the dim hum of the air conditioner.

"I've had enough, now and forever," the thin woman said, pulling at strands of her short gray hair. Her body quaked with some form of indignation. "The obscenity of it—this girl, this man, this *sewer*. Profanity, the vileness of it. What this girl does with her pussy is her own business."

The woman rose—rather, leaped up. *"Scum,"* she said to the populace.

Out she went, gone in a fraction of a moment, her tense presence swept away by her misplaced fury.

"Well now," Jesse said, trying to bring the episode to an end, "what's for dessert?"

DR. FELIX MARTINEZ came to Jesse's room about an hour after dinner.

"I understand you handled yourself well and took care of a tough moment at dinner," he said.

"How do you know that," Jesse said, sitting up in bed, reading *The Magus.*

"That's why we're here," Martinez said, with what Jesse took to be a touch of parody.

Dr. Martinez, a handsome dark-skinned man with long fly-away black hair, looked to be Jesse's age. He spoke in a deep voice that suggested an older man, or at least, to Jesse, an older face. The face at the foot of his bed was collegiate, and delightfully unprepared for politics. His eyes were merry and unskeptical, as far as Jesse was concerned.

"Olsen was taking liberties," Jesse said about his absent roommate.

"That's Mark," Martinez said with a chuckle.

"You have all the details?" Jesse asked.

"It's common, Mr. Savitt, I can assure you."

"Any truth to Olsen's claim?"

"I'll give you a surprising answer: maybe," Martinez said, showing Jesse a sense of theater by dramatically isolating the "maybe" from the rest of the sentence.

"So *that's* Julie's Achilles' heel," Jesse said.

"Don't jump to conclusions," Martinez said with a sudden but irrevocable formality. "It's not your concern."

"If I displayed even the slightest interest in the matter, would that brand me as an opportunist?" Jesse said, making friends.

"You see your choice of words, 'brand.' Who do you think we are, your enemy?"

Before Jesse could answer, Olsen came into the room with a Slinky.

"Good evening to one and all," he said, taking a seat on the side of his own bed, using the Slinky as an accordion.

"This man told me he was a nitwit," Jesse said. "How much truth is there to this, Dr. Martinez, or is that not my concern."

"I'm no nitwit," Olsen said indignantly, but with little energy. "Where'd you get *that* idea?"

"If you'll recall, you told me precisely that, just before dinner."

'He's the nitwit," Olsen said, pointing an index finger at Dr. Martinez.

"Well now, the worm turns," Jesse said, smiling at Martinez conspiratorially.

"Gentlemen, I'll leave you for the evening," Dr. Martinez said.

"Could you just tell me the itinerary for tomorrow?" Jesse asked.

" 'Itinerary' is not a word we use," Martinez said.

"Well then, routine, schedule," Jesse said.

"You may want to rest," Martinez said.

"Do I look tired?"

"I don't know you that well," Martinez said, from the doorway.

"May I have some sleeping medication?" Jesse asked.

"They'll be around with it," Martinez said.

"What kind," Jesse asked.

"So, we have a pharmacist here," Martinez said.

"Think of the possibilities: Valium, Librium, Seconal, Tuinal, the great veteran phenobarbital, or perhaps the genius of Nembutal."

"I'll just tell you this: it's in liquid form."

"In a tiny little paper cup," Jesse said, as much to himself as to Martinez. "Why liquid?"

"It's a deterrent to storage," Martinez said, and raised his hand in farewell to both patients.

"You've been more than forthcoming," Jesse said. "Olsen, where'd you get that Slinky?"

"In Recreation," Olsen answered, spreading the Slinky wide.

"How often do you have your treatment?"

"None of your business," Olsen replied, without anger.

"Let me ask you something, Olsen," Jesse said, picking up *The Magus*. "Did that girl Julie really show you her twat?"

"I wouldn't say it if it weren't true," Olsen said with a goofy grin. "She just dropped her pants."

"What did *you* do," Jesse asked.

"I just stared."

"What color twat."

"None of your business," Olsen said.

"What color twat," Jesse repeated.

"Brown," Olsen said with that goofy grin of his.

"Why would she show you her twat," Jesse said.

"Because I'm handsome, and, unlike certain people I know, I'm not a fag."

"What certain people," Jesse said, watching their progress with amusement, but unable to subdue a sudden cloud of anger.

"It's all agreed on the floor," Olsen said, with the situation well in hand. "You're a fag." Olsen was really working the Slinky.

"You mean there's been a discussion about it?"

"There's been a meeting of the minds," Olsen said.

"If that's so, I'm in no danger," Jesse said, turning to *The Magus*.

"And what exactly is *that* supposed to mean?" Olsen asked, halting his Slinky play.

Jesse paused, understanding his choices.

"Fag," Olsen blurted out.

"Fellow," Jesse said, "relax."

"That's what all fags say," Olsen said.

"Olsen, shut up," Jesse said, without raising his voice.

"You shut up, you fag," Olsen said, resting the Slinky on the floor.

Olsen got up and went to the door.

"Fag attack!" he yelled into the hall.

In seconds, Martinez materialized.

"This guy made a pass at me," Olsen said to Martinez.

"What do you think, Dr. Martinez," Jesse said. "Do you think he's got a case?"

"What exactly did he do?" Martinez asked Olsen.

"He went down on me," Olsen said, returning to the bed, to the Slinky.

"And you let him?" Martinez said.

"There was nothing I could do. He overpowered me with a knife."

"Where's the knife?" Martinez asked.

"He put it in *that* drawer," Olsen said, pointing to the middle drawer of the bureau closest to Jesse's bed.

"Let's have a look," Martinez said, walking across the room.

From the designated drawer, Martinez removed an open pocket knife.

"This yours?" Martinez said to Jesse.

Jesse stood up. "Now, come on. I've never *owned* a knife. That's clearly not my knife. You took everything away from me, including my shoelaces. How could I have a knife? What would I *want* with a knife?"

Jesse heard himself as unpersuasive.

"He went down on me," Olsen said.

"OK now, this is enough," Jesse said, getting really angry.

"Calm down, Mr. Savitt," Martinez said coldly.

"This asshole belongs in a loony bin," Jesse said, creating an immediate silence.

"I'll take the knife," Martinez said finally. "The lights go out at nine, you know," he said to Jesse, who searched his face for help.

"Can't I see Emerson before Monday?" Jesse asked.

"There's always help on the floor," Martinez said as he left.

"Let's just be quiet," Jesse said to Olsen. "Let me read, and I'll let you Slink."

Soon, sleeping medication was brought in.

The lights, centrally controlled from somewhere in the building, were turned off about fifteen minutes later.

Jesse lay on his back in the dark with his eyes open. He thought unemotionally of Jessica Morelli's bloody temple, her rapid and efficient exit—"I pity you, Jesse Savitt."

"Fag," Olsen said.

BY SATURDAY AFTERNOON Jesse had read *The Magus* twice. He lay on his bed, watching Olsen sleep, listening to thunder announce the imminence of a storm.

He got up and went to the window.

From the third floor, he looked down at the stream of cars on the parkway, a blur of travel; trouble-free citizens with destinations and radios and chewing gum, not inflicted with the likes of his own hostile heart, arranged in groups of friendship and devotion, with a firm grasp on the steering wheels of their lives. Baseball fans, music listeners, moviegoers, so unlike Walker Percy's solitary moviegoer in his endless string of darkened auditoriums. Jesse wondered about Percy, trapped in his Southern humidity. Was he an elegant guy with an extravagantly civil tongue in his head? Clearly spiritual, was he a family man, hearth-obsessed? If Jesse went down there to New Orleans and sought Percy out, and told him what he'd done to Jessica Morelli, told him about the rope across Fifty-seventh Street, told him many, many things, would Percy offer forgiveness? Was forgiveness in his Southern cards? If forgiveness was not in his Southern cards, then how could he have written *The Moviegoer?* But, no go, Jesse thought. Percy was a theologian, Jesse was a wrongdoer without a theological thought in his cranium. Percy would be gently dismissive. Jesse would be back in New York before he knew what hit him. Better to stay away from Walker Percy.

Olsen stirred, his eyes opened. He offered a loopy grin. Jesse thought he was about to say something, but Olsen closed his eyes and turned his face to the wall, like Jessica Morelli on the couch, Jessica, naked from the waist up, accepting Jesse's ministrations, a representative of Luna come all the way East. Quite a catch. Luna would laugh at the likes of Jesse Savitt. Orlando the genius would order him off the premises. Jesse wondered what kind of premises. Was it an office building? A private house? A sprawling campus overlooking the Pacific Ocean? Whatever the premises, Orlando the genius would order Jesse off it. Orlando and Walker Percy, in different parts of the country, would turn Jesse out.

Who would not? At this point, in this late summer heat, who would find Jesse a singular guy, a positive contributor, a desirable presence?

Jesse's only relative had been told about Dr. Armstrong, and Riverdale, and the Undetermined Length of Stay. In Longchamp's, where they had sat, Norman Savitt had gravely lowered his head.

"Why do you feel this is necessary?" he had asked.

"Because I'm in a muddle," Jesse had replied, the letter that he had written to his father in an inside pocket of his seersucker jacket, never to be handed over.

"But why not see a psychiatrist?" Norman had asked.

"I'm not medically covered, except through hospitalization," Jesse had told him.

Norman hadn't responded. He had looked past Jesse, his gaze fastening on something behind his son's chair.

"Maybe it'll work out," Jesse had said.

"You know I'm with you."

Jesse knew that. Who else but Jesse could Norman be with? These two stumbling people had no one else to call.

"And that I love you," Norman had added.

"Me too," Jesse had said.

"Are you completely convinced it's the best course of action?" Norman had asked, receiving lentil soup from a woman too old to be working.

"No. But it's a course of action."

"What can *I* do?" Norman's eyes were filling with tears.

"Don't *blame* anybody."

"There's no one at fault, I know. I know."

"It's a peculiar time," Jesse had said.

"But I'm not pessimistic," Norman had said, after a pause.

"Me neither," Jesse had said.

JESSE WANDERED OUT of the room and down the hall.

He saw Julie Sargent reading in Recreation.

Felix Martinez was on the phone in the nurse's center. Jesse heard him use the word "illusionary."

Jesse went to the men's room. As he sat in an open cubicle the sound of rain began.

He washed his hands and returned to the hall.

Suddenly, and without a plan, he slammed into the bar of the emergency exit door, setting off a deafening alarm.

Quickly, he was down the stairs.

Malcolm Anderson was in the lobby.

Jesse swept by him and out into the rain.

Jesse was off, out of breath fairly soon, but he kept on running, tumbling down the hill in the mud, reaching the Henry Hudson Parkway. He could still hear the alarm at the top of the hill, though it appeared that no one was on his trail.

He ran along the side of the parkway, gasping for breath.

He veered right on an exit ramp, as if he were a vehicle.

The rain got heavier, the sky blacker.

Jesse kept going, soon finding himself on upper Broadway.

He stopped for a moment under a skimpy tree by the side of the road. He was aware that he wasn't thinking, that his version of consciousness had shut up shop. He was simply on the fly, into Van Cortlandt Park, across two baseball diamonds, into the woods east of the fields, and finally under a copper beech tree, at last out of the rain.

He lay on his stomach, regaining his breath.

He slapped his backside, checking for his wallet.

Confiscated, of course. He didn't have a dime—only, remarkably, his key chain.

At 242nd Street, Jesse waited, then passed unobserved through the subway exit gate.

Covered with mud and rain, he took a seat in the first car of the next outgoing train.

He waited impatiently for about five minutes, until the doors shut, opened, shut again, opened, and shut.

Jesse closed his eyes.

In a moment, he got up and went to the front of the car, standing alone, watching the tracks, the dilapidated old stations into which they pulled, the tunnel way down there at Dyckman Street that was coming ever closer.

And soon the darkness of the underground, Jesse facing his own reflection, and the yellow signal lights turning green in the natural flow of events. Out again at 125th Street; the rain had turned to drizzle. And then back down to stay, under Columbia, under the Riviera Theater, under Zabar's and the Ansonia, and Columbus Circle, and the Colony record shop, and Times Square, and Penn Station.

Jesse got off the train at Twenty-third Street.

HE USED HIS key to Maxine's apartment.

Maxine was in bed, tangled in the arms of a man Jesse didn't know. The man's waist-length blond hair had gathered with Maxine's own long blond hair to cover her face.

"It's me," Jesse said, observing Maxine's obscured vision.

"Hey," the man said conversationally, groping for the green sheet.

"How do you do," Jesse said. "Max, I need money."

"Jesse, this is Owen," Maxine said, unconcerned about her nudity.

"How do you do again, Owen," Jesse said. "You'll get it back in a week," Jesse told Maxine.

"Owen's a friend," Maxine said, sitting up to face Jesse. "One would hope."

"Where'd you get so dirty?" Maxine asked, leaving the bed.

"I got caught in the rain," Jesse said.

"Hey, man," Owen said, his inflamed genitals at long last concealed.

"I can make you out a check," Maxine said, not hesitating.

"I need a quick shower," Jesse said.

"How much do you want?" Maxine asked, sitting naked at her desk.

"Two hundred dollars, and a little cash, if that's possible," Jesse said, undressing.

"It's in the account," Maxine said, appearing to grasp Jesse's unusual urgency.

In the shower, Jesse rinsed himself clean, and shampooed with a bar of Maxine's black soap.

When he pulled back the shower curtain, he found Owen facing him, wearing underpants.

"You and I are about the same size," Owen said most gently. "You take my clothes, and I'll take yours later on, when they're dry."

"That's generous. That's sweet. Thank you," Jesse said.

"It was Maxine's idea," Owen said with a smile.

Maxine appeared in the bathroom door. "Here's a check, and a twenty," she said, extending it all to Jesse's wet hand.

Jesse took the money and put it on the laundry hamper.

"You'll have it back in a week, I promise," he said, drying himself. "I've never had such a large audience for this. Herzog hated to dry himself."

"Who's Herzog?" Owen asked, now standing above the toilet bowl.

"A fictional character," Jesse said. "I always think about him when I'm drying myself."

To Jesse's surprise, Maxine turned on the water in the sink and began to brush her teeth.

"One minute I'm in a soaking rain, the next minute I'm

plunged into an actual little family," Jesse said, feeling tenderly about Maxine and Owen. "You guys know each other a long time?"

"We met, when was it, Maxine?" Owen said. *"Juu*ly," he continued, adding splash to the event.

Tara slipped into the room.

"Tara-bara," Maxine said through toothpaste lips.

Tara coiled around Owen's right leg, and blinked up at Jesse.

"Everything's under control," Jesse said to Tara, thinking that Tara remembered Jessica Morelli's accident, and the smell of blood, and the flurry of towels and washcloths.

Owen flushed the toilet.

"What do you do?" Jesse asked him, drying his toes.

"Psychiatric counseling," Owen replied with authority.

"Honestly?" Jesse asked, slapping Maxine on the behind.

"Yup," Owen said.

"Great," Jesse said.

"He's really good at it. That's how we met," Maxine said, just before rinsing her mouth.

"In other words, you sought him out," Jesse said, wrapping a towel around his waist. "I didn't know that."

"I needed guidance. I *need* guidance," Maxine said.

"Max, I honor that in you," Jesse said.

"You want some chow?" Owen asked, leaving the bathroom.

"I've gotta go," Jesse said, following Owen out.

"Jesse, if you'd like, you know . . ." Maxine said quietly.

"I'm late," Jesse said to her, over his shoulder.

"For what?" she asked, trailing them both.

"I'm not sure," Jesse said, stopping, allowing Maxine to catch up with him. He put his arm around her waist.

"Hi, honey," she said, looking up at him.

"Hang tough, sweetheart," Jesse said. "You'll get more and more support from me. Guidance. Yes, guidance. But I can assure you I won't usurp Owen's territory."

"That's OK," Maxine said. "I think most of us need all the help we can get."

HE TOOK THE subway home.

His apartment was in disarray, as he had left it. Roaches raced over the dirty dishes in the kitchen sink—Jessica's midnight supper, unresolved. Summer dust had gathered in all of the rooms, and a gray afternoon light intensified the muskiness of his quarters. Tara could still be there, brandy could be flowing, the house in crescendo, Jesse heading briskly to Jessica Morelli's stinging conclusion.

Jesse called his father and got no answer.

He changed from Owen's clothes to his own.

He made a drink, and called his father again, to no avail.

He waited for the rain to stop, and then went out, climbing the hill of 100th Street up to West End Avenue, and on to Broadway.

Broadway between 100th and Ninety-sixth streets.

No connecting tissue on *that* journey. Everything gone wrong, despair leaking from buildings like oil spills: dirt-streaked windows filled with the eyes of dead fish, the light green of cheap corduroy, the mirthless eyes of televised actors in silent triplicate; and all along the way, frantic Latin music rolling out of stifling pizza holes, the general concert of fury.

Jesse took the subway to a midtown liquor store that would cash Maxine's check.

He attended a porno film for a half hour, unaffected by a

robust blond woman who lay on a couch in a living room setting with an actor Jesse had recently seen on the Eighty-sixth Street crosstown bus.

At six-thirty, Jesse went into a Blarney Stone for a whiskey.

He watched the news, imagining his day recounted: a hand-held camera in the men's room in Riverdale. That same camera following him down the hill in the mud, along the side of the parkway, above him as he lay on his stomach beneath the generous copper beech tree, behind his right shoulder in the front of the IRT subway car, and then the discovery of Max and Owen, after Jesse's departure an interview with Max in her charming nakedness: "I absolve Jesse Savitt, and I only hope he's caught before he's cruel again. This is my friend Owen dressed in Jesse's clothing. Please don't mistake him for Jesse. *He's* a guide and a counselor and a companion."

Jesse walked over to Madison Avenue and took a bus to Ninety-fourth Street, heading for his father's apartment.

As he reached the corner of Fifth and Ninety-fourth his father emerged from his building with a woman Jesse had never seen.

Jesse ducked away, out of sight.

From a distance, wounded, he followed them down Fifth Avenue. The woman held his father's arm. They strolled intimately.

At Eighty-ninth his father hailed a cab.

Jesse was left alone by the Guggenheim Museum. He slid down into a sitting position, his back against the wall of the museum.

Ten minutes later, Robert F. Kennedy, wearing a pin-striped suit, walked by, with a man Jesse didn't recognize.

"Hi, Senator," Jesse said. "You've caught me at a weak moment."

Kennedy, misunderstanding, replied: "Thanks, and good luck."

In a while, Jesse took the Eighty-sixth Street crosstown bus, hoping for another glimpse of the porno actor. As he left the bus through the front door he said to the driver: "Thanks, and good luck."

Jesse walked up Broadway, stopping for a plate of spaghetti in a little Italian restaurant.

In his bed, in the dark, he repeated over and over: "Night falls fast / Today is in the past."

He made two questions out of it.

"Night falls fast?"

"Today is in the past?"

Had *that* ever occurred to Edna St. Vincent Millay?

Later on, near dawn, Jesse realized that he had the same initials as Julie Sargent.

9/11/67

Jesse boy,

Are you all right? Please contact me. The hospital phoned up and said you had left without a proper release. You must have given them my number and my name. They said they felt that you needed attention and that they had evaluated you extensively, but that your action was unprecedented for them and that they couldn't welcome you back. I'm just paraphrasing their letter because I have it at home and I'm in my office. They said that you left of your own accord on September 9, which was Saturday, if I'm not mistaken, and so I'm going to send this letter by messenger to you, so that if you are at home you'll receive it today (Monday) and you might feel like getting in touch with me, as I worry about you so, but I don't wish to interfere with your life or to barge in on you on the telephone or in person. I know that you need your privacy and that you must have had some reason for your action. I know that a psychiatric hospital isn't exactly a cottage by the ocean. Also, I wanted to tell you that I would be very open to assisting you financially in private therapy, if you would like to pursue that avenue. I think it is very important that you receive advice or professional help, or whatever the terminology is, and though you may feel reluctant to borrow or to simply take money from your dad to this end, I would hope that you would take into account my love and devotion to you as my dearest and only son. You made your mother and me very proud when you were a little boy with what everyone considered a very highly developed creative instinct, as manifested in the stories you composed and the stories you told both your mother and me, and in the stories you mailed to us from the dormitory when you were ten and eleven and twelve years old, and the stories that, long after your mother's death, you sent to me when you were living in Europe, and when you were in California.

And even though things haven't gone perfectly for you in recent years, and you may think that by using my financing for your therapy you are showing yourself to be less than an adult (something with which I don't agree), I do believe, my dearest son, that you have the talent and the *will* to succeed at whatever you choose to do. Sometimes it takes certain gifted young men longer to find an outlet for what they do best, whatever that may be, whether they are musicians, as I am, or lawyers or writers, or whatever field of endeavor they are attracted by, and sometimes these late bloomers, as they are sometimes called, overtake the early starters with richer and far more meaningful work than the wunderkinds are ever able to produce.

This is not a despairing time, though you may think so at the moment. Do you remember that relationship you had with that brilliant young girl who was a novelist at nineteen or some such improbable age? What has *she* done recently? And do you remember how you despaired when the relationship ended, and you drew a cartoon in the style of David Levine, the cartoonist, that showed you standing on an enormous scale looking obese and unkempt, and above the numbers on the scale was the word WORTH, and you had the scale indicator pointing at the number ZERO? Well, you felt pretty low at about that time, didn't you, but you rebounded, giving me great pride and joy, and I remember wishing your mother had been alive to see you overcome adversity and get on with your life, as you did many times when you were little, believe me. (The running away from camp summer—do you remember? You were able to work it all out in a very well written story that you called "Orange Pea Soup." Do you remember? You sent us that story in Beverly Hills, in 1951, I'm certain.)

So, you see, adversity takes all different forms, and never fully comes to an end. Certainly you know the adversity in my own life. I don't need to go into it here, and I point it out only to show you how adversity never tires of its pursuit, which is the testing of the human soul. You are being tested now in your frustration, your inability to get things really going in the field of your choice, and in other areas I can only guess at. I hope you will accept the help I gladly offer, and that you will not see me as an interference, or, as your mother used to say so many years ago, an ogre. Please, my dearest son, contact me to reassure me that you are all right, as the note from the hospital has filled me with concern.

Your loving dad

My Dad,

Your worried and wonderful letter is here before me, and I want you to know that I am Fine. To meet me on the street would be to meet a reasonable fellow. No one would think of the word "lunatic" after such a meeting. Nor would I. Nor *am* I. Please be assured that the light at the end of the tunnel is *not* the light of an oncoming train, but a *real* light, a luminosity made of expectation and quiet. I'm not an expert in these fields, but I've *heard* of the fields and have the directions in my pocket. Spacious fields, I'm told, with a consistent and endurable climate.

A couple of things in your letter were of special interest to me. That young writer, the girl. You kind of ask what she's been up to. The fact is, she died in Sloan-Kettering last year. I hadn't seen her in a long time, then I heard she was sick, then I heard where she was, then I heard she died. Sally Gleason. I once told her that I felt she was living her life upside down in a mirror. I'm sure that was the case when she died in the hospital. Sally Gleason dead. Bald, no doubt, and upside down. Before she knew me, she had had an affair with a famous psychiatrist who was treating her, a much older man who committed suicide. Do you remember the name Leonard Goltz? He jumped from the roof of 1095 Park Avenue and landed right next door to Dalton at the start of the school day—8 AM or so—and many of the kids saw this happen. I think it's possible that you have imagined me in Goltz's role, searing the psyches of a bunch of fourteen-year-olds on the way to school. I am here to tell you that nothing could be further from the truth. My own special complications are not made of Sally and Leonard. They are made of a distorted vision; to be more specific, a *double* vision. I seem to be viewing a split screen, which activates both my intelligence and my indolence, occasionally together, most often individually. The indolence allows for cheap indiscretion, pranks of all kinds, vivid little undisciplined dramas without any spines. I become boneless, a human cutlet. With my intelligence in tow, the indolence becomes diluted by thought, even reason, and the impractical little jokes are less likely to take to the podium. At the very least, there's a delay mechanism at work. I buy time to consider my options. My intelligence, let loose from any encumbrance, will always deal me a good hand. *That's* the reasonable fellow on the street that one is likely to encounter. So, you see, I am not about to consider calling my life a day, what with all this common sense on the page.

"Orange Pea Soup." What would *you* have written after being forced to stand in front of about a hundred for the most part moronic and brutal thirteen-year-old boys in the mess hall of a summer camp in the State of Vermont in the middle of a heat wave to be judged unanimously (by voice) guilty of ignoring the camp rules by leaving the premises, unattended by an authority? And then you are lustily booed by the ensemble. I'll bet you didn't know that, you on Cañon Drive, me in Bunk 17, in Asia.

"Daddy, today at lunch I was booed."

"Who booed you?"

"Everybody. The whole camp."

"That's terrible."

I mean, what could you have said from Cañon Drive?

"Orange Pea Soup" is a great and cynical title, don't you think? So there you go.

Did you know that your son is kind? It's true. I am deeply

kind in my innermost self, *all the time.* It's the split screen that causes trouble, where some oozy substance, like the ink from squid, crawls across the kindness, blocking my view of the game. Someone has stood up in the row in front of me. A tall guy with a cup of beer in his hand. A real fan.

I did notice the use of the word "extensively" in your letter, as in "they had evaluated you extensively." I had a twenty-minute talk with a doctor named Emerson, and bits and pieces of dialogue with a doctor named Martinez. And you're right about it not being a cottage by the ocean.

The truth is: I feel *kindly* toward those people, toward the other patients, toward the whole rickety setup. Sometimes I am ashamed of my kindness, the kindness in my heart. There are times when I behave unkindly, overcompensating as I am. But I believe that everyone's piece of the action is honorable, is worthy, is stunning and unique. The whole ball of wax is sensational, and *that* is an overcoming realization.

You and I will stand by each other in the years to come, empathically reading our own histories. If we look skeptically at our future, we will do so at the expense of real Quiet. Quiet is where kindness flourishes, and that is my commitment to the family that we are. You and me. Less noise from my side of the room, if you please, my father is trying to read.

Love,

Jesse

FAITH

"Molly, look," Jesse said.

They were standing on the balcony outside the Top of the Strip restaurant on the twenty-fourth floor of the Dunes Hotel, anticipating a late-August hurricane. It was midday. The dawn had been clear—Molly and Jesse had watched it, wrapped together in bed, finally quiet after hours of talk. During the morning the sky had turned gray with large black ovals embedded within it, hanging like stars of death, moving quickly in an increasing wind, replaced by others. "Black holes," Molly had said on the balcony.

Jesse was pointing down to the Olympic-size pool, to a man he recognized, even from such a height, as Vernon Prager, swimming his familiar laps, though the pool was closed, his access to it probably gained by special permission, the result of many trips to the Dunes Hotel, where Jesse had run into him once before. His path was straight, disciplined by a thousand hours in pools the world over. In private clubs for men, at a YMCA in Chicago, at the Sonesta Hotel in Key Biscayne, he would persist, goggles pressed tightly over his eyes, his course intruded upon by frolickers and backstrokers gone astray and the directionless floating of the legally blind. Vernon never changed his course, Pummeled by other swimmers, he continued: a hundred laps. Other bathers sensed the rage. Their own light spirits tempered by caution, they acquiesced, giving Vernon room. His autonomous laps ruled the roost. When at last he emerged from the water, a muscular graying man in his late forties, his hair matted to his scalp, goggles in hand, his severe countenance suggesting disdain, a hush would fall in the shallow ends until the imposing body, disengaged from the pool, disappeared into the showers or steam rooms or down the tiled steps to the beach.

On the balcony, Jesse told Molly about Vernon Prager: the editor of a national magazine, once an excellent fiction writer—his two novels were among Jesse's favorites—and a solitary world traveler, no longer married, childless, a voracious consumer of paperback thrillers, literary, territorial, needy.

"I care for him, if you get my point," Jesse told Molly. "I care for him because he's austere, and because he's sad."

"He's probably oblivious," Molly said.

"True," Jesse said. "But his mind is alert, like someone trapped in a stroke. He looks paralyzed, but his brain is thinking a blue streak."

"What's it thinking?"

"Probably: I can't help you because as you can see I can't move a muscle."

"Why do you hang around him?" Molly asked, trying to light a cigarette in the wind.

"I don't really hang around him. He's such a good editor of my pieces. Any journalist'll tell you that."

"But is that sufficient?"

"Are you *judging* me, as usual?"

"Why do you take umbrage so easily?"

"Because you've never truly let me alone."

"Do you want me to leave?"

"See, now you've invented a whole different issue so that you can be assured that I *don't* want you to leave, that I need you. You go to the brink with your tests, you know. One day somebody's gonna throw you off a balcony."

They didn't say anything for a while. They focused on Vernon Prager in the empty pool.

"Should we look him up?" Molly asked.

"Maybe," Jesse said.

Molly slid her right hand along the railing until it touched Jesse's left hand.

"I didn't mean to judge you," she said softly.

"But it just comes out," Jesse said, debating whether to go on with it.

"We're solid, aren't we?" Molly asked.

"We're more than Vernon has, I'll say that."

"DEAR MOLLY," JESSE had written on June 1, two months earlier, "You could be miles away now—Israel, with some guy named Chaim. I see him: bearded and intense in this 1974 summer, wanting to talk karma with you and eat berries for eleven straight days. Israeli berries, huge and sour things busting with cleansing items going through your system so you can use all those words with Chaim, like pancreas, spleen, colon, and, of course, cervical area. How the Food Is Affecting Molly. Tell him about Jean-Claude's retreat. Mountain berries cleansing your liver and kidneys and, oh yes, cervical area. You can work them all in and Chaim will sit before you and love you in Israel. And that's where you could be right now, except I know you're not. When somebody loves somebody, they keep an eye on somebody's whereabouts, somebody's sexual whereabouts, somebody's lower back and spine and cervical area. So I know you're in New York in that ridiculous maid's room of an apartment, and that you directed a play that lasted close to four hours, and that your work was called spare, economical, all the words you like. No fat in the production, and no fat on the director. 114 pounds, am I right? Lean, tight, Winstons (and I'll bet that you still think that twelve Israeli berries will neutralize 7000 Winstons; I have always noticed that you seldom use the word 'lungs').

"I'm interested in peace with you. Enclosed is money for a plane trip to where I am. To where you *know* I am. The California desert has succulent berries, cleansing berries. I have a little house. I miss you. Standing next to you is like standing in clear broad daylight, as in a Spanish town at noon."

Molly hadn't replied, hadn't shown up, hadn't given intermediaries a clue. But she hadn't returned the money, which Jesse knew to be her reply. He had shopped for Winstons and berries, and when, at last, she had phoned from the airport eleven miles away, waiting, she had said, "in this unfeasible heat," he had raced to her in his rented Colt, with only an AM radio and springs popping out of the backseat. They had stood facing each other in the baggage area, taking a look at each other for the first time in four months, for the first time since Molly had moved out of his apartment in New York City on Valentine's Day.

That summer, Jesse wrote a piece on forest fires; Molly went with him to Pendleton, Oregon. Jesse wrote a piece on the California Angels; Molly went with him to Anaheim. Jesse wrote a piece on the murder of a middleweight boxer; Molly went with him to San Antonio, Texas.

They fought once, in the desert, Molly on her back on the floor clawing at Jesse's face, Jesse above her, shaking her. Molly had said that because she was with Jesse and not in New York available for work, not doing work, not directing in the East, she was losing her reputation, her career. She was losing money. Then she had said: "You owe me twenty thousand dollars."

They listened to music: Dylan, jazz, Samuel Barber. They watched Nixon leave office. They watched him address his staff, watched him depart along a red carpet. Molly observed the contradiction.

One night Jesse said to Molly: "You're getting to look a little like Margaret Hamilton."

One afternoon Molly said to Jesse: "Avedon couldn't yank cheekbones out of that flaccid round face of yours."

One Sunday night Jesse said to Molly: "You're a tough cookie." Molly replied: "And you're half-baked."

In Pendleton, Oregon, Jesse said to Molly: "I think we're hopelessly involved with each other because we're hopelessly frightened of each other." Molly made no reply.

In San Antonio, sitting by a murky stream that wound through the center of town, Molly said: "I see evidence that you're becoming your father."

"What evidence," Jesse said, taking a bite of his bean burrito. They were dining outside a filthy snack bar that had come highly recommended by the grieving wife of the murdered middleweight boxer.

"It's in posture and expression," Molly said. She had limited herself to guacamole and chips; a piece of tomato skin had stuck between her two front teeth.

"Are you suggesting I'm decaying?" Jesse said, taking Molly's chin in his left hand and wiping her teeth with his right index finger.

At a nearby table, an obese woman dressed in pink said to her audience of three: "They'll never be able to reconstruct the nostril."

"Not decaying, I didn't mean that," Molly said. "There's a certain tempo to your speech, a gesture—your hand a moment ago when you were talking about Haldeman—I guess an attitude. I see my mother in me. She's much more pronounced in me than, let's say, ten years ago. My question is this: do you think that as we become our parents as manifested physically and in, as I said, attitude, do you think we see the *terrain* like they do, or did, or something? I mean, do we agree with them politically, or do we feel as they do about endive or Streisand? Is it possible that, in a given situation— I'll make it a real question. In a given situation, do we have *exactly* the same take? Are we frightened little bunny rabbits over *exactly* the same things? Are we as secretive, and in *exactly* the same ways? In other words, how deep does the merger go."

Jesse didn't respond for a moment, partially stuck with the unreconstructed nostril as he rummaged through Molly's words, wishing to organize them perfectly. He succeeded before she repeated them.

"The truth is, the sad truth is, I don't know my father that well," Jesse said.

"He plays it close to the vest," Molly said, "as, in certain ways, do you."

"He's a theatrical man," Jesse said. "He's a poseur in a different way than I am. I don't have elegant flair."

"But the times don't call for elegant flair," Molly said.

"But they demand sleight of hand. Maybe, in retrospect, I'll look as Cole Porterish as my father does now."

"My mother's panic is your father's pose," Molly said.

The woman in pink said: "A little bit goes a long way."

"Do you want the rest of my burrito?" Jesse said.

"No," Molly said.

Jesse got up and went over to the woman in pink.

"My dear," he said, noticing Molly turning away, embarrassed, "would you care to have the rest of my burrito?"

"How spontaneous," the woman said, her arm extended, accepting Jesse's plate.

———————

IT BEGAN TO rain late in the day. Jesse left Molly propped up in bed reading *The Biochemistry of Memory*, and went downstairs to wander through the casino. He recognized a television comedian at one of the roulette tables, surrounded by an enthusiastic entourage of three men and a woman. "What did Jesus say to the Polish people?" the comedian was asking. "He said, 'Play dumb till I get back' "

The entourage crumbled with laughter. The woman slipped an arm around the comedian's waist.

Jesse lost twenty dollars at another roulette table. He liked the feel of chips, the clickety sound of the roll, the extravagant colors crowded together in so small a space. He called Molly from a house phone to tell her this.

"Do you know what I just read?" she said. " 'The brain is the stomach of the soul.' "

"In *The Biochemistry of Memory*?"

"No, I switched. Nabokov."

"Do you think Nabokov was meant to be read in Vegas?"

"I would think he'd say Vegas most of all."

"Come down and play with me," Jesse said.

"Later."

"Reading isn't a *job*, you know. Why do you make everything a task?"

"I'm not making a task."

"Wait right there. I'll buy you some Nietzsche at the newsstand."

"You know, Jesse, everyone doesn't have to be just precisely as frivolous as you."

"We've never had an argument on a house phone."

Eventually, Jesse drifted into the Savoy Room, and slid into a booth for a hamburger.

"You can't sit there," Jesse was told by an approaching blond woman in charge of the Savoy Room.

"Why?" Jesse asked, knowing why.

"It's a booth for four. Please be good enough to use a booth for two." The woman carried an open menu that she withheld from Jesse.

"Madam," Jesse said, not fully decided on tenacity, "as I see it, I am one of five customers in this coffee shop at this moment. In addition to this table for four, there are—let me take a wild guess—fifteen other tables and booths for four. The tables and booths for two are for midgets and children. Let me be more specific: they are for children who *are* midgets, whose parents were or are midgets. Midgets down through the ages, stretching back centuries. Thousands and thousands of midgets to whom your tables for two would seem commodious. May I stay seated here at this comfortable table for four?"

"You may not," the woman said, closing the menu, the issue.

The gesture, its finality, got Jesse angry.

"I think you're going to have to get professional men of law in here. Policemen, security. In the meantime, I'll just see what's in these little pink packets in the sugar dish. I don't think I've ever seen pink packets before, have you?"

"You will not be served," the woman said. She turned and

walked away, assuming a hostile position near the cashier, facing Jesse, watching him tear open ten pink packets and the regular packets of sugar, adding salt and pepper, and finally water, and ice cubes with holes in the middle. Then Jesse wiped his hands with a napkin, and stood. Passing by the cashier and the hostess, he said, with a warm smile, "Excellent. The best in the West."

The reply, to Jesse's surprise, was in Spanish, from the hostess. Its tone told of detestation. With his back to her, Jesse raised his arm and waved his hand in farewell.

In the casino, Jesse felt tears somewhere. He called Molly again.

"I won fifty dollars at roulette," he said.

"Wonderful!" Molly said.

"Is it raining?" he asked. "There aren't any windows down here."

"Pouring. Utterly pouring," Molly said. "And the wind. We're having a real hurricane."

"Are we having a good time in Las Vegas?"

"Sure we are, sweetie."

Jesse spotted Vernon Prager watching the baccarat.

"What do you think you'll want for dinner?" he asked Molly.

"Do you want to have dinner with your friend?" Molly asked.

"Maybe," Jesse said. "But maybe he's checked out."

"In a hurricane?"

"Well, there's always the Dome of the Sea. Fresh frozen fish."

Jesse realized that Vernon's appearance way across the room had turned him sentimentally to Molly.

"I love you," he said into the house phone.

"Ah," Molly said.

VERNON PRAGER'S DOUR expression changed not at all at the sight of Jesse.

"Hello, Jesse," he said, as if they had traveled to Las Vegas together and had spent the afternoon apart. In fact they hadn't encountered each other in three years. Vernon's hair was grayer, and he looked thinner. He had established a gaunt and haunted face, angular and severe. Jesse thought: Sorrow without wit—though he knew Vernon to be occasionally hilarious as he revealed the troubles of his adventures. It was this prospect, Jesse realized, that had encouraged him to confront Vernon and extend a dinner invitation, presenting Molly with the gift of Vernon's comic despair. Vernon's unanimated greeting hadn't fazed Jesse; by now it was familiar. Jesse had received it before: in a casino, in Vernon's office on Sixth Avenue, at a publication party upstairs at the Russian Tea Room, and at a hot dog stand in Madison Square Garden. He had seen other people wilt at its starkness and pull away, injured. Vernon was inhospitable, reclusive, cold. His contempt was constant but low-pitched and easily deflected in polite society, where Vernon seldom lingered for anything more than a handful of salted nuts. He would return to his furnished fifth-floor apartment, bearing manuscripts and galleys. The apartment itself, a gray two-room dwelling, unatmospheric, hotel-like in its melancholy neutrality, was distinguished only by a hundred toy soldiers that Vernon had arranged on a Formica desk, and by a framed color photograph of an attractive dark-haired woman about forty, dressed in a wet suit, holding goggles similar to Vernon's. He called this woman "my circus girl," because of her athletic prowess and ubiquity: a diver; a skier; a roller skater; a tennis player, tournament bound in perpetuity; on the phone to Vernon from clubhouses and gymnasiums, one who perceived Vernon as a father and adviser—Rebecca Casey, Vernon Prager's girlfriend.

"I see you've come to your favorite place," Jesse said, watching the baccarat alongside Vernon.

"This trip has been filled with travail," Vernon said.

"You seem none the worse for wear."

"But I am," Vernon said. He turned and addressed Jesse directly. "Essentially, I'm a ruined man."

"Would you like to have dinner with me? With us, as a matter of fact. I'm here with a girl named Molly."

"It would have to be at seven. I'm still a walking New York clock, and I'm stumbling through an eerie time zone of discontent."

"Sure," Jesse said. "What with the storm and everything, how does the Dome of the Sea strike you? At least it's in the building."

"I've always found it peaceful there. But then again, that's how I find Vegas." Vernon smiled for the first time. His face softened for a moment, before returning to the cold. In that moment, Jesse saw Vernon in Truro in 1962, emerging from a lake with a beautiful woman named Anita Long. Anita had accompanied Vernon on his marathon swim, three times around the lake. As they came ashore Anita had taken Vernon's hand, igniting the very smile Jesse had just received. Jesse thought of taking Vernon's hand right there by the baccarat tables to force another little gift from Vernon's unyielding eyes.

"Molly and I saw you in the pool today. We were up at the Top of the Strip," Jesse said, instead.

"That swim is a significant part of my travail," Vernon said bitterly. "I hope you won't find eating with me unpleasant, what with the story of my dismaying trip."

"Not at all, Vernon," Jesse said. "You're always gracious in defeat."

"Laugh if you will. My story will devastate."

"I understand," Jesse said.

BACK IN THEIR room, Jesse watched Molly shower behind a translucent door. He recalled her showering out of doors at a beach house, her hair a hat of shampoo, her eyes closed to the suds, her thin little-boy body circling under the water like a carousel. She was made perfectly for him, ribs visible even behind a translucent door, her skin desert-brown. Her eyes were always focused intensely on the projects of her life: the application of lotions, the preparation of bluefish, the arrangement of flowers, the pages of Chekhov. She was the second of three daughters, her father a biochemist, her mother a teacher. All of her Lexington Avenue childhood had force-fed jobs to be done, goals to be reached. Molly, now twenty-eight, flew through her days, lithe and muscular, leaping from task to task, leaving the ground in flight, "like an acrobat," Jesse had pointed out. Words came tumbling from her, cascades of ideas and accusations in an alluring deep voice through a commanding vocabulary. A woman of the theater, of ball-point notes and black coffee and pumpkin seeds and Winstons.

"I think you'll like Vernon," Jesse said. "Or at least enjoy him." He was lying on the bed watching television with the sound off, and watching Molly dry herself.

"What will I enjoy most about him?" Molly said.

"I think his cadence. He speaks in rhythmic sequences that become very literary passages. He speaks as if he's rehearsed everything, but let me assure you it's not dull. I think lucidness relieves his tension."

On the televised news a car on a London street exploded. In the bathroom, Molly leaned down to dry her calves and feet.

"No one would think of Vernon as endearing," Jesse said, "but he's not sinister. He's blue. The sonofabitch is blue."

"What do you think he'll think of me?" Molly asked, pulling white slacks on.

"The best in the West," Jesse said.

"What?" Molly said.

"He'll like you," Jesse said.

"What about the East?" Molly said, dressed only in slacks, her hair wet, her feet bare.

"Ah, well, tootsie, in the East you just might leave something to be desired."

"Am I too serious for him?"

"What I said, my love, was flirtatious."

"Far too obliquely for my particular taste," Molly said, stopping at the side of the bed to watch another silent televised explosion.

"HOW COULD THIS happen to me?" Vernon asked, nursing a Coke as he waited for swordfish.

The three of them were sitting in the Dome of the Sea while a large-bosomed blond harpist slid back and forth in a rowboat on tracks in the center of the restaurant displaying copies of her own record album at the stern and bow. Molly had added an orange T-shirt and sandals to the white slacks. Jesse observed that she had fallen quite nicely into Vernon's sorrow, making him comfortable. Indeed, Vernon addressed *her,* occasionally flicking a glance at Jesse, eventually leaving Jesse in the dust as he talked.

"Tell me in detail," Molly said, smoking a cigarette, leaning forward a little, all ears.

Vernon took her on as his audience. Jesse, unthreatened, felt comfortable in his invisibility.

"Here are the things that have gone wrong since I left New York by taxi early this morning."

"In chronological order," she said unfacetiously.

"Firstly, the plane departed Kennedy twenty-five minutes late due to an unfathomable malfunction which was never explained. Secondly, my arrival at the hotel, late though it was, was still a premature arrival in view of the fact that the room I care for, room 1520, was occupato, if you know what I mean. The room they had assigned me— and, by the way, strictly entre nous, I had booked 1520 twenty-five days ago, a usual habit and an effective one— the room they had assigned me in the Olympic wing wasn't made up yet, and I was asked to return in an hour. All this time, all these many years, coming here, tipping generously, behaving in an exemplary fashion, and I am told, *peremptorily,* to return in an hour. It's fifteen minutes after twelve—I beg your pardon, *earlier.* You see, I had discovered that I had left my watch on the plane, just so un-*like* me. The Savoy Room is jammed, the casino is filled, the humidity is high—and I learn by overhearing conversation that a *hurricane* is due. A *hurricane,* mind you. And my wandering reveals that the Olympic pool is closed, for no discernible reason, and I am forced to go to Major Riddle's office to ask permission for its use. The Savoy Room, when I finally gain entrance, has run out of onion soup, and serves tomato juice, for the first time in my memory, with ice cubes, watery little ice cubes. Don't laugh at me,

Molly, when I tell you that I would never have come had I known what was to befall me."

"Hadn't you known about the hurricane?" Jesse asked.

"Do you think I would have been so foolish as to fly across the country to arrive here in what I consider a quite remarkable sanctuary if I had known of a fly in the ointment? One as menacing as a hurricane? I am meticulous in preparation, and I was fooled completely by the current conditions." Vernon sipped his Coke, shaking his head sadly.

"Go on," Molly said, resting her fingertips on his wrist.

"I'm a rigid man, I'll admit that," Vernon told her, "and I do expect far more than what can ever be delivered. I thank you for your compassion."

"Why Vegas?" Molly asked, removing her fingertips.

Jesse noticed the familiar drinking man's tremor in Vernon's hand, though Vernon had always been essentially abstemious. Jesse had occasionally considered that tremor, not daring to bring it up with Vernon. Something neurological, perhaps—it stretched back to Truro, where Jesse had first spotted it; perhaps the result of thousands of hours of editing, of gripping pencils and creating small marks on manuscripts, composing paragraphs in margins, working in miniature through the thirty years of his adult life—a semicolon tremor, most understandable. Now, at the Dome of the Sea, could that tremor be saluting Molly's touch, her wisp of skin setting off infatuation?

"Why Vegas," Vernon said, including Jesse for the first time in a while, gathering in everyone for something he felt was important.

"I have my reasons," he said. "They are these: Firstly, I can eat comfortably and in quiet at the Savoy Room."

"I'll give you that," Jesse said.

"Secondly, the Olympic pool is of proper size and temperature for my swimming habits. Thirdly, there is much to overhear. There is a sense of benign panic from which I am immune. It's a very beautiful city."

"Well, then, nothing could be insurmountable," Molly said, offering Vernon a cigarette. To Jesse's surprise, Vernon accepted it.

"I know," he said somewhat mournfully.

"You seem to be caught up in the malfunctioning of small things," Jesse said, wishing to make a contribution.

"The fact is, I have no attachment to people or causes, nor do I have any particularly outstanding ambition. I have no faith, and I have no nagging regrets that this is my lot. For me, it's the minutia that delays the way to indifference, something I'm most comfortable with. If a trip is to be made to a designated area and the arrangements are elaborately coordinated in advance, then I truly expect professionalism in the carrying out of those arrangements. I am, on a daily basis, disappointed by incompetence, broken promises, false advertising of a personal nature, all of which cannot be overlooked without considerable heartbreak. I'm interested in a certain kind of trashy American fiction, and also in specific British authors. It's always been my goal to find myself alone and unbothered by the nuances of friendship or romance. That's why Vegas is so hospitable to me. I'll bet you that I am one of the very few men who have come here time and time again and never dropped a dime or a quarter into a machine, or stepped up to any table with chips in hand, or received a pair of dice from a croupier."

They fell into silence, Molly and Jesse immersed in Vernon's outpouring.

Vernon, who had lit the cigarette and taken a puff or two before putting it out, drew a cigar from an inside pocket of his seersucker jacket and lit up, supplying the table with a ceiling of smoke.

Their silence was interrupted by the arrival of dinner.

"It doesn't look very appetizing," Vernon pointed out with an unexpected smile, one that made Molly smile. "But still," he went on, "during a hurricane you're lucky to get fed."

"HOW DO YOU pass the time, aside from swimming? Without gambling." Molly took a loud bite of an apple she had brought with her to the table. Through the years, Jesse had found rice cakes in her shoulder bag, slices of egg whites in aluminum foil, bite-size chunks of grilled tuna in Ziploc bags, Tic Tacs, packets of herbal tea, grapefruit, avocados, cooked artichokes, handfuls of chocolate Kisses, pumpkin seeds like sand at the bottom of every bag.

"I follow the pornography industry," Vernon said.

"I didn't know that," Jesse said, his arm in the air, signaling the waitress for a drink.

"At the risk of being indiscreet, I can tell you that my relationships with certain profiteers in this particular field have never been better." Vernon sat back, pleased.

Jesse imagined that the juxtaposition of pornography and Molly was, for Vernon, pornography itself.

"Have you fallen in with the *actual* people?" Molly asked. With the waitress at her side, Molly, uncharacteristically, ordered a brandy.

"No," Vernon said. "I'm far too anonymous a figure to risk it. It's just that there are specific merchants in the larger cities—Miami, New York, Los Angeles—with whom I've struck up more than a casual conversation. I'm welcomed in a way that probably suggests friendship to the other shoppers, or, shall we say, strollers, consumers."

"How do you account for it?" Jesse asked.

He found the incongruity of this tragedian drifting boldly, *conversationally*, into porno shops both impressive and amusing. Jesse himself, with an expertise born of study and purchase, had always browsed unobtrusively from behind sunglasses. "Pick 'em out, fellas" didn't bother him in the least. He would fade casually out of the store and into another, raising no objection to even the most Teutonic instruction. His search was surreptitious. He felt himself in no danger.

"It's a somewhat commonplace voyeurism," Vernon said, not at all uncomfortable in front of Molly. "I believe I have a kind of harmless demeanor that I affect under those conditions," he continued, lighting up another cigar. "I ask about business, about the newest sexual accoutrements, and I display a professional interest that suggests comradeship rather than prurience. I have been asked on more than one occasion if I myself was in the business. You work up a certain knowledge and it shows."

"I gravitate to bondage," Molly said, stunning Jesse.

"You *what?*" Jesse said.

"That's right," she said. "Every now and then."

"Have you ever bought anything?" Vernon asked.

"No. But no isn't the issue."

"Would you care to do some shopping?" Vernon asked Molly.

"Jesse?" Molly said.

"Conditions aren't perfect," Jesse said. "There's this hurricane."

"How far is it?" Molly asked Vernon.

"On a June night we could drive it in eight to nine minutes," Vernon said.

"Do you know *exactly* where to go?" Jesse asked.

"My dear man," Vernon shot back almost jovially, "do you know who I *am*?"

VERNON HAD NO car.

"I've been too exhausted to deal with the renting process," he told them as they left the restaurant.

"But you know the roads," Jesse said, calling for his own rented car.

"Naturally," Vernon said, standing inside the Dune's entrance for a moment to stare out at the storm.

"Is this advisable?" Molly asked them both, without much weight behind her words.

"We'll creep along," Jesse said.

"I have to take a quick shower," Vernon said.

"Why?" Molly asked.

"It's a personal discipline," Vernon replied. "Don't upset yourself, I'll be here in twelve minutes."

Molly and Jesse walked through the casino, their arms around each other's waist. "I don't really find him as cynical as you think he is," Molly said.

"Would you call him hopeful?" Jesse asked.

"I wouldn't go that far," Molly said. "He's very attractive in his eccentricity. You know what he is? Loveless. That's what I get the most from him. But loveless isn't hopeless. For a sour ball he's a decent guy."

They stopped to watch a lounge singer, a man of about fifty, wrestling with "This Could Be the Start of Something Big." Jesse imagined his mother, miraculously alive twenty-two years after her death, tap-dancing as lounge entertainer with himself at the piano grinning cunningly at an elderly audience. "Sometimes I'm happy / sometimes I'm blue / my disposition depends on you." His mother, in the pink suit she'd worn on V-E Day, would smile at him as she danced. He remembered going out to dinner on V-E Day. He was five, and had been taken along to a restaurant for a celebration. At the table, his mother, falling ill, had crumpled onto his father's shoulder and then dropped into his lap. Tiny white dumplings had fallen onto her pink suit. Jesse had seen it as a dizzying signal of joy, a custom, among many, with which he was unfamiliar.

"Did you know my mother was a singer?" he asked Molly.

"Yes. And her favorite song was 'Lover.'"

"I don't remember telling you that," Jesse said. "Where were we when I told you that?"

"I'll tell you exactly where we were: we were walking on the beach in Sagaponack over the Fourth of July, 1970. Our first outing. I remember everything you told me that weekend."

"Has everything held up?" Jesse asked.

"Don't be ridiculous," Molly said.

Vernon was waiting at the bell captain's desk.

When they set out, torrential rain made it difficult to see more than a few feet beyond the hood of the car. A tough head wind prevented anything but a crawl.

"Las Vegas Boulevard South," Vernon mused, from the backseat.

"This is folly," Jesse said.

"Nonetheless," Vernon said.

They made their way cautiously, Jesse clinging to the right lane, progressively more concerned as they sloshed forward in the increasing flood.

Vernon directed, "Turn right on Charleston."

Jesse noticed through the rearview mirror that Vernon

appeared to be having a good time, relaxed and seat-belted, his legs crossed as he held an unlit cigar. Jesse thought it possible that Vernon's deepest pleasure, contrary to his rigidity, would only be realized at the edge of some cliff; that nothing but the prospect of an actual abyss would comfort him. And tantalize him. So far down there to the valley. An endless drop to the rocky basin. No more *imagined* catastrophe, no more private demons slashing at his heart. Only the real thing could mollify Vernon Prager.

Were he to lose his balance and crash to the rocks, would those relentless laps memorialize him? The sheer endurance of it all, the ten-dollar tips at the Sonesta Hotel's pool, the papers of special permission, the goggles snugly in place, the sureness of stroke, the deflection of the legally blind, the phone calls of praise and wonder from Rebecca Casey.

In their silence, Jesse imagined Molly sharing these exact thoughts. How intimate that would be. And how absolutely out of the question. She then would have known of his mother's pink suit, and the dumplings. She would have been able to hear his mother singing in the living room, his father at the piano, a Hamilton piano, with a Miró above it: "Miró, Miró, on the wall," his father had often said, to new groups of listeners. And his mother standing in the curve of the piano: "Lover when I'm near you and I hear you speak my name / softly in my ear you breathe a flame."

Perhaps five miles down Charleston Avenue—Jesse wasn't sure, so fearful was he of taking his eyes off the road—Vernon cried out: "There!"

Jesse pulled off the avenue, inching through a deep accumulation of water. Attacked by the windblown downpour, they ran from the car and were soaked in seconds. With their backs to the rain they stumbled their way the few

feet to the porno shop. A large yellow sign on the door read
UNDER SEXTEEN IS A NO NO.

Inside, creating puddles, Jesse said to Vernon, "I think NO
NO should be hyphenated." And to a fat man in a red cotton
jumpsuit at the counter by the door: "What's your view on
this?"

"Pardon?" the man replied.

"I think NO NO needs a hyphen," Jesse said.

"It's for them who's underaged," the man said. "You got
the place to yourself."

Jesse had never enjoyed the run-of-the-store. He had always been one of a group of slithery patrons, his eyes frozen
on the possibilities before him. He was now able to leisurely
ascertain that in this particular fluorescently lit little room,
care had been taken to separate the hetero from the homosexual matériel; that bestiality had a wall to itself; and that
the display of real intercourse occupied the three racks most
easily overseen by any proprietor.

"Penetration," Jesse said to Molly.

"The caviar of the industry," she said.

Jesse observed that the pictorials of simulation were no
less expensive. It seemed that the final glossy thrust, financially evaluated at no higher a figure than the fakes on the
opposite wall, were still acknowledged, by placement, to
contain the heart of the matter.

Vernon had moved away from Molly and Jesse, dripping
his share of the storm across the orange linoleum.

"What's this about bondage?" Jesse asked Molly.

"You never knew?" Molly said with a smile.

"No," Jesse said. "Are you kidding, or what?"

"There's something to be said for being trapped. Held
down."

"I didn't realize that that translated into sex for you,"
Jesse said.

"Only superficially."

"It's interesting how many wild ideas stir up the loins."

"Honey," Molly said, taking Jesse's hand for a moment, "that's exactly where world wars are conceived."

"Look at this," Vernon said from across the room.

He came over to them with a book called *Making Sister Happy.* "Read this paragraph," he said. "You can read it out loud, it's far from offensive."

Jesse read: " 'Kathy didn't know what to do. Her terrible problems were sadder than she thought possible. That night she dreamed of her family reunited by the seashore. Someone had made sandwiches which they all shared under a red-and-blue umbrella. Her father tossed her a hard-boiled egg. She dropped the pieces of shell into the sand. Her mother smiled and offered her some chocolate. When Kathy awoke she had the taste of eggs and chocolate in her mouth, the taste of Easter. She began to cry.' "

"C. B. Williamson," Vernon said. "I've never come across his work."

"Could be a woman," Molly said.

"Published by Nightstand Books," Jesse said. "Copyright 1972."

Talking on the phone, the man at the counter said: "All them apples ain't worth zinc."

"Does it have raunchy stuff?" Molly asked.

"I don't know," Vernon said. "I just opened it to this page."

"Someone should buy it, on behalf of Williamson," Jesse said.

"We'll each pick out something. My treat," Vernon said.

When they left a half hour later, they left with Molly's D. H. Lawrence; Jesse's blatant pictorial, *Valerie;* and Vernon's cluster of Nightstand volumes.

"That's Annette Havens, you know," Vernon said, pointing to Jesse's magazine.

"How do you know her name?" Molly asked as they stood at the counter.

"We're dealing with Vernon Prager," Jesse said. "Doesn't that tell it all?"

INCHING THEIR WAY back to the Dunes, Molly said, "We were in there for an hour."

"Time flies in a good bookstore," Jesse said, withholding his growing concern about the drive.

During the hour the rain had intensified and the wind had strengthened. Jesse felt that he was on the brink of driving blind.

Vernon, in the backseat, had lost his joviality almost as soon as he had buckled up. He had fallen into a potent silence that made Jesse feel guilty. Jesse rummaged through his feelings, locating the guilt but not its roots. Molly lit a cigarette and sat with her legs tucked under her, as if she were at a campfire.

"This is the toughest going I've ever seen," Molly said conversationally.

"When you come right down to it," Jesse said, "this isn't much good."

"Do you think we should pull off and just wait it out?" Molly asked.

"We'd be sitting here all night. I think the thing to do is to actually get *back*."

No one spoke for a while. Molly shifted her position, dropping her feet to the floor.

"This is outrageous," Vernon finally contributed from the back.

"Are you blaming us?" Jesse said, annoyed.

"What's blame got to do with it?" Vernon shot back. "We're in trouble."

Seconds later, almost on top of Vernon's remark, Jesse found that he was tailgating another car, that he was inches behind it, that it didn't seem to be moving. Jesse veered right and went into a skid. He braked, throwing Vernon forward. The car slid down a modest embankment and came to rest on a paved service road. In the process, Jesse's right arm automatically extended, pressing Molly's waist, acting as an additional seat belt, keeping her secure.

"I can't go on!" Vernon yelled.

Jesse turned, to find Vernon's mouth bleeding. He had banged his lip on the back of Molly's seat, but was coherent.

"It's cut, that's all it is," Molly said, ministering to Vernon with a handkerchief.

Vernon grabbed the handkerchief from Molly's hand and crushed it tightly to his lip.

"This is fiendish," he said.

"We're OK, we're OK," Jesse said.

"What does 'we' have to do with it," Vernon continued, spitting words and blood into the handkerchief.

" 'We' means everything's OK," Jesse said coldly. "It specifically means that Molly's not hurt. You dig?"

"Don't give me this 'dig' crap," Vernon said contemptuously. "I'm not a sophomore."

"You missed its true spirit," Jesse said.

"You're Ok, Vernon, you just cut your lip," Molly said, on her knees on her seat, facing him, trying to help.

"You informed me you were a quality driver," Vernon

said, taking the handkerchief away from his mouth to examine the damage.

"The subject never came up!" Jesse said. "It's a fucking hurricane, we all agreed to make the trip. What are you after?"

"Peace of mind," Vernon said, in a softer voice than before.

"I'm tired of you," Jesse said suddenly, surprising himself.

"That's what one gets for extending friendship," Vernon said, with a special kind of sorrow in his voice that irritated Molly.

"Are you totally blind, or what," she said without inflection.

"This is the limit of my endurance," Vernon replied, checking his teeth with his fingers, finding less of a blood flow than he had apparently imagined.

"Pull yourself together," Jesse said.

"Of all the shabby things to say," Vernon said, almost under his breath.

Jesse chose not to acknowledge it. Instead, he turned to the immediate project of movement, finding the car was in order, finding that he was able to see well enough to navigate back onto Charleston Avenue. Reversed as they were, having spun around during the slide down the embankment, the wind and rain now lashed at the back of them, allowing Jesse a meager visibility.

Once reinstated, Jesse drove Charleston, and then Las Vegas Boulevard, at ten miles an hour. Wishing to regain at least a flake of friendship, taking into consideration Vernon's role as editor and employer, Jesse offered the suggestion of an apology by saying to Molly, "I didn't see the guy."

"Honey," Molly said, resting her hand on Jesse's arm, "I know that."

"As disappointing an excursion as I've ever participated in," Vernon said, still checking his teeth.

"It had its jolly moments," Molly said, helping Jesse out.

"Well at least you have your *Valerie,*" Vernon said icily.

"I'm grateful to you," Jesse said sarcastically.

They didn't talk for the rest of the journey. Jesse stole an occasional glimpse of Vernon through the rearview mirror. Vernon's eyes were downcast, his chin resting on his chest as if he were trying to sleep. Once again Jesse remembered him in Truro twelve years earlier, rising from that lovely lake in victory, Anita Long at his side, goggles in his hand, a cloudless August day spattering them with summer colors, accenting sex. Jesse, envious on the shore, had yelled out, trying to latch onto a piece of their shimmering good fortune: "Watching you swim was spellbinding." If they had heard him, they hadn't shown it. Instead, they had dried themselves with bright red beach towels, saying things to each other that Jesse, fifty feet away, couldn't hear. Now, in the car, the thought of "spellbinding" made him wince.

In the lobby of the Dunes, Vernon examined himself in the first available mirror.

"It doesn't appear to be dreadful." He spoke as much to himself as to Molly and Jesse.

"I'm sure there's a medical department, a medical room somewhere," Molly said, holding Jesse's hand.

"It's unnecessary, I can assure you." He still held the bloodstained handkerchief.

"Your books," Jesse said, noticing their absence.

"I left them in the car," Vernon said. "But no matter. I'm far from being in the mood for trivial fictional characters."

"I can understand," Jesse said.

"But at least I have *Women in Love,*" Molly pointed out, with a gaiety that pleased Jesse.

"And I *Valerie,*" Jesse said, implying conclusion, good-bye.

"When are you leaving?" Vernon asked Molly.

"In the morning," she said.

"Perhaps I'll see you in New York," he said without a smile.

"Maybe things will go better for us in an urban setting," Molly said.

"I would think," Jesse said. "We strayed too far from our element."

"What do you mean," Vernon asked.

"I don't know," Jesse said. "Just fool's talk."

"Jesse meant we'll see you soon."

"That's it exactly," Jesse said.

BY DAWN THE rain had stopped, though the wind remained forceful. Molly and Jesse, lying in bed, watched pages of newspaper and ribbons and hats and a single yellow balloon fly by their window. The clouds were breaking, allowing splashes of sun to soften the early morning.

"Everything seems so green," Molly said.

Jesse had room service deliver breakfast: French toast, fried eggs, fresh strawberries. He put on Mozart, a chamber music cassette, and held Molly in his arms until breakfast came. They sat together at the rolled-in table, Jesse's chair the foot of the bed.

"There are people in this building with dice in their hands at this very moment," Jesse said.

"They think it's late afternoon," Molly said.

" 'Benign panic,' I think Vernon said."

"And also: 'It's a very beautiful city,' " Molly said.

"What if he was right," Jesse said. "What if it turned out,

after many surveys and investigations and expert evaluations, stuff like that—what if it turned out that he was *right.* That Las Vegas, Nevada, is, aesthetically, the most beautiful American city. Its streets, its boulevards, the colors of the walls in the casinos, the fluorescence, people's clothing, just *everything.* And that we had it all *wrong.* All these years. Paris was a dump, Florence an assault on the senses. Just a complete reversal of human observation, human taste. With big-time guys agreeing with the findings. Aesthetes, artists, Renoir sprung to life, *agreeing.* Vegas is the most beautiful spot. Not only American spot, but *the most beautiful spot on the face of the earth. And no one argues!"*

"Maybe later on, down the road," Molly said, pouring coffee. "A hundred and eighty degrees from now."

After breakfast they went back to bed. Molly fell asleep for a half hour. Jesse woke her up by placing the palm of his hand on her nose.

"Do you think little planes will be flying?" he asked.

"Call," Molly said, almost asleep.

AT NOON, THEIR packing was easy: cassettes and T-shirts and moccasins and Molly's makeup and *Valerie* and D. H. Lawrence.

"That was a decisive evening," Molly said as Jesse counted his cash.

"It'll have a bearing," he said, not looking up.

They walked down a long carpeted hallway together, Molly's arm around Jesse's waist.

"This is never-ending, like the Dallas airport," Jesse said.

"Jesse, look," Molly said.

They stopped at a window that provided a view of the

Olympic-size pool. The solitary swimmer, goggles in place, was Vernon, somewhere in the middle of a hundred laps. The storm had blown chaises longues and pool chairs and large sun umbrellas and magazines and newspapers into the water. Vernon swam through it all, bombarded on all sides by the chaises, furiously swatting at them with his hands. They floated in front of him. They crashed into his feet and legs. They encircled him. He lashed back without missing a stroke, using his sides and thighs, making progress.

Molly and Jesse watched for a while in silence, then continued down the hall.

Nearing the lobby, Jesse took Molly's hand. He spoke in a soft voice.

"Ah, Vernon," he said, "keep the faith."

DAY
TRIP

Nancy and Simon came to visit Jesse in the California desert. Jesse had rented a little house with two bedrooms for the spring and maybe the summer. "I am leaving you irrevocably, do you get the point of *that?*" Molly Malick had said in New York in February. A Danny Kaye film was on television with the sound off. Jesse had glanced at it just after Molly had said what she said. Molly had also said, "We are small personalities, if you really want to know the truth." Then Jesse had told Molly some things about herself that were quite uncomplimentary. Molly had said the word "irrevocably" again, repeating it over and over while Jesse spoke. Then she had left the apartment and had spent the night with her friend Beverly, and the next day, in his absence, she had moved all of her things out of Jesse's apartment. Now it was May 18, and not a word had passed between them since the night the Danny Kaye film was on television.

On April 1, Jesse took some books and cassettes and flew to Los Angeles. He bought a used car and drove down to the desert and stayed in a hotel until he found something suitable to rent. He spent a lot of time listening to and reading about the Watergate hearings. He disliked Nixon's lawyer, James St. Clair, and wrote two intemperate letters to him at the Boston law firm with which he was associated. Jesse was embarrassed that his own address included the word "palm," so he changed it to "parm," hoping that if St. Clair replied, the post office would spot the error, reading "palm" for "parm," and deliver. St. Clair didn't reply, or the post office couldn't make head or tail of "parm," even with the correct zip code, or maybe Jesse's letters were intercepted at the law firm and discarded.

Jesse also sent a postcard to his father that pictured the home of Liberace.

April 26, 1974

Dearest Dad,

It's raining so hard today I can't see the mountains. Most unusual for this time of year. People here are arid. Their eyes are dead. Parched retinas. I'm constantly thinking Murine! Get Murine! Language serves only the act of request, and a specific kind of uninteresting courtesy. That's the California desert for you. I miss a good old ruthless New York face. It seems to me that long ago you cultivated a very sweet looking anticipation. Sometimes you appear to be looking forward to something—or you'd have us believe that—maybe your next knockout of a score.

With my love, of course,
Jesse

Jesse used the phone a lot, especially in the early morning between six and eight. He spoke to friends in New York and in Boston, four or five of them several times a week, to his father once a week, to Simon every so often. Simon was coming to Los Angeles to work on a film, "to co it," Simon said, meaning to co-write. His collaborator, Nicholas, the director, edited reclusively, insatiably. Nicholas was serious in his aloneness, but was never accused of showboating.

"Nancy is in Nicholas's film," Simon said, introducing her to Jesse.

Nancy was fair, with long blond hair and wide blue eyes. She wore a bonnet and a sleeveless white dress. Even as she removed her bonnet and sat down a radiant smile continued on.

"Drop your face," Simon told her.

In one second the smile vanished. Nancy's face, in repose, looked weary.

"The energy this girl puts into keeping that vast warmth," Simon said with a laugh. "The tension of the face muscles." Simon sat down on the couch next to Nancy and patted her knee, with no condescension that Jesse could pick up.

"Simon told me about you in the car," Nancy said.

"Well," Jesse said, hearing what he might have said ten years earlier: What did Simon say? Tell me *exactly*. I mean *everything*. The point being: does he respect me?

Jesse had learned that Simon could easily spot him warming to his theme. Simon was on the ball right from the start of anything. So now, early on a Friday evening, Jesse simply said, "Well."

Nancy glanced at Simon. Jesse saw that she was looking to him for approval. For what? For the way she sat, with her hands in her lap? For telling Jesse he'd been spoken of in the car? Was she so crippled, so entirely needy? These were usually the people Simon quickly discarded. He was willing to soothe and medicate, or accept a few anemic jabs at the heart, but would push no wheelchair around. Regardless of blue eyes and absolutely perfect good looks.

"Put the TV on," Simon said. "They think they've found Patty Hearst."

Jesse, who hadn't been following events that day—he'd been straightening up and shopping, working for Simon's approval himself since sunrise—was surprised to discover some sort of televised shoot-out.

"The end of the SLA," Nancy said.

How rich and satisfying her voice was, geographically neutral, pleasantly theatrical.

"Tell us what's going on," Jesse said to Nancy, eager to hear her speak.

"They've got the last of the SLA in that house, including Patty Hearst. It's the end of an era," Nancy said, surprising Jesse with her overview. Perhaps it was Simon's overview in the car, and Nancy had stolen it outright. Jesse thought that that wasn't likely; she would never deliver it as her own in front of him; Simon could call on so many sources of punishment. It was, then, her own idea: end of an era. This drama on live television that they were watching with the sound off was a metaphor. Jesse thought: Maybe Simon will die here. Jesse found pleasure in the possibility. Overcompensating, he leaned down and gave Simon a hug around the neck. "What can I get you?" he asked. "There's all the fruit you want. Cheese. Something to drink. Anything at all."

"Do you have any orange juice?" Simon asked, after thinking it over. While Jesse poured the juice, Simon lit a joint.

"It's dynamite stuff," Nancy said, accepting the joint from Simon.

Simon smoked grass and cigarettes all day long. He had graceful feminine hands that dealt flawlessly with matches. He was tall and reed-thin, and always dressed shabbily in loose long-sleeved army shirts and baggy jeans. Most of the time he wore moccasins. At thirty-three, his short brown hair was showing traces of gray. He had a long nose and black eyes. When they had first met, Jesse's nickname for him had been the Devil. "Ah, the Devil," he would say, when Simon called or came around. Jesse knew that Simon Mandel was a comet of destruction, sweeping into sight now and again, telling people the truth with malice to burn, and then shooting away, out of sight, leaving great gashes of spirit, leaving men and women in many ports sitting at their desks writing letters of apology to Simon Mandel, pages and pages of explanation—classmates from Harvard, Hollywood associates, a woman who wrote children's books, one or two or three or all of his five sisters, various members of several schools of enlightenment scattered from Rio de Janeiro to London to San Francisco, and Jesse Savitt, concealing his letters from Molly Malick, who didn't buy Simon. "Who do you think you're writing to—God?" she had said when she found the pages in Jesse's drawer.

"It's a lot more complicated than you think," Jesse had said.

"Simon the truly spiritual," Molly had said with disgust.

"You don't have any respect for people's privacy," Jesse had said.

"Yes I do," Molly had said. "I needed a pen and that's where I simply saw—"

"You cheat on important rules," Jesse was reduced to saying.

After they had watched the silent television screen for ten minutes or so, Jesse said, "How can they be sure?"

"Of what?" Simon said, taking the last toke of the joint they were sharing.

"That Patty Hearst is in there."

Simon paused, inhaling, and then he sat, thinking. Simon

often took a long time to reply to a question. Jesse felt that in that time Simon was in debate with cruelty, wrestling with a constant fury, trying to prevent it from leaking into placid waters.

"Of course, we're not listening to the commentators," he finally said.

"At your request," Jesse said.

"It might very well be that Patty has nothing to do with this, and isn't around, and isn't even watching this, and is having a meal, perhaps some kind of pasta, with an iceberg-lettuce salad and a creamy dressing of some kind."

"What do you mean?" Nancy said. "I don't get it."

Jesse looked for Simon's eyes so that they could join together at Nancy's expense. They had done this often, richly condescending, slashing away in silence at whoever they thought was impoverished. This was when Jesse loved Simon the most, when they were a team, when the shorthand was theirs alone. What made Jesse wary, what made Jesse scared, was the very real possibility of a turn of events that would place him, abjectly, in the seat of the fool. It occurred to Jesse, as he met Simon's eyes, that all of those sisters and associates and enlightenment scholars and writers of children's books were after the same elusive diamond: Simon's accepting attention.

"I mean that Patty's probably got a hunger on," Simon said. "It's dinnertime, time for chow, hasn't eaten all day, except for some Saltines, two or three maybe, a little grub, a little chow, a piece-a-nourishment, a little nosh."

"A chocolate bar, not Saltines," Jesse said, getting right in line.

"Oh, I see," Nancy said.

Simon put his hand on Nancy's knee and kept it there, not allowing Jesse everything on the table. Nancy put her hand over his and kept it there, joyously, Jesse imagined; in fact, there was even the suggestion of that radiant smile. It was entirely possible, he thought, that this girl was too absolutely stunning to refuse, no matter what came out of her mouth. Could it be that Simon was willing to push a wheelchair up an incline simply for a photogenic face?

"Maybe there's a movie on," Nancy said.

———

THE NEXT DAY they took a hike in Andreas Canyon. It was an easy climb, around and occasionally through a trickling stream born of the melting winter snows in the mountains. They leaped from rock to rock, slid under fallen palm trees, following a trail the Cahuilla Indians had provided. They rested on the smooth rocks by a modest waterfall, sharing a can of Coors. An hour later, deeper in the canyon, they smoked grass by a larger waterfall and watched two teenagers, a boy and a girl, swim naked in an icy pool in the rocks. A cassette player hung from a limb of a tree, presenting a tinny version of George Harrison's "My Sweet Lord." It was a hot desert day, from which all the climbers were partially shielded by the palms. Farther on, out of George Harrison's range, in a small moist cave, they ate bologna sandwiches.

Jesse told Simon about Molly. Mostly, Jesse *told* things to Simon, who seldom asked questions. Jesse knew that many people were anxious to spill their beans to Simon so that he might fix things on the spot; it was unnecessary for him to ask anything to get things started. He would just sit around, smoking grass and cigarettes, and he'd get all the stuff he needed. Jesse considered Simon ungenerous, though others had often challenged this. "Ungenerous?" the children's book writer had said incredulously. "Who gives *more* to people? More time, more compassion, more *commitment!*" Jesse felt that Simon gave no commitment, none at all, but he had kept that to himself.

"So your dilemma is how to reconstruct your life with Molly without losing the balance of power which is in your favor, which made the clock tick in the first place." Simon took a bite of his sandwich.

"Yes," Jesse said, "I'm afraid that's true." He hadn't been talking about power, but Simon had put his finger on it.

"Have you talked with her?"

"No."

"Do you love her?" Nancy asked earnestly.

Do I love Molly Malick? Jesse thought.

Parading his oppressive and violent love for Molly in front of a beautiful young woman who, he had come to think, might be accessible down the road would be counterproductive. He felt that Nancy's naive respect for a love so utterly titanic, so maniacally territorial, would preclude his lurid wooing in some as yet undisclosed ballroom.

"I have," Jesse said.

"You mean once, or what?" Nancy said.

"Jesse and Molly have intense complications," Simon told Nancy.

Simon often stood in for people, supplying decisive punctuation and crucial information, shutting down lines of questioning.

"That's right," Jesse said.

"Yes. Well, it's just that Nancy is unfamiliar with the saga," Simon said.

Jesse wondered if "saga" minimized or elevated. Simon, frequently a neutralist, could, for the sport of it, downgrade from above the fray.

"Do you feel I've made too much of it all?" Jesse asked.

"Now, Jesse," Simon said with a smile. "We love you for your excesses."

Jesse said nothing. The "we" and the "excesses" were too much to grapple with.

"Does anyone want to go for a swim?" Nancy said, finishing her sandwich.

"Why don't you," Simon said.

"All by myself?" Nancy said, standing.

"We'll look after you," Simon said.

The cold water in the pool outside the cave tested Nancy's courage. Sitting naked on the rocks, she dipped a foot in, withdrew it, tried again. She was ivory-white, and, to Jesse's surprise, voluptuous. In a while she was in, splashing, quite at ease. "Come on, you guys," she shouted, to no response.

"How old is she?" Jesse asked Simon.

"Twenty-three," Nancy shouted.

Molly Malick was twenty-eight. Jesse imagined her in the pool, treading water, laughing, making her way across the pool where she could stand, holding out her arms to him, spreading her arms to him.

"You know," Simon said, "you could respond to Molly."

"Respond to what," Jesse asked.

"To the current conditions," Simon said.

Nancy got out of the water and stretched out on her back on the smooth face of a large boulder.

"I'm in trouble deep," Jesse said.

Simon lit a joint.

"That's powerful stuff," Jesse said.

"I live mostly underwater," Simon said. "So who am I to advise anybody for or against anything."

LATE IN THE afternoon, deeper in the canyon, they fell asleep on fallen palm leaves. A distant siren signaled the end of the day at five, but they didn't hear it, though there had been warning signs along the trail. When they awoke it was nearly six.

"What can be done to us," Jesse said.

"I would imagine someone will extract some sum of money," Simon said.

They made their way carefully down, past their cave and Nancy's boulder, moving back and forth across the stream, following the trail. Rattlesnakes watched them rigidly from the brush. Small iguanas scurried out of their way.

"This is a cute hideaway," Nancy said.

"I'll bet that's what Patty was thinking," Jesse said, with less disdain than he felt.

They reached the car a little before eight. A mile down the road they were stopped by a metal bar locked into place across their passage.

"We're trapped," Jesse said, pleased by the complication.

They all got out of the car to examine the possibilities.

The rocks on either side of the road prevented circumvention. Simon fooled with the lock on one side of the bar. Nancy sat on the pavement, her chin resting on her knees.

"How far would you say it is?" Simon asked Jesse.

"I'd say five miles. We'll leave the car, and I guess come back."

Jesse imagined Molly with him, just the two of them, happy with this. They would hold each other right here in the road, and share a warm beer.

Simon started up another joint and passed it around. Then they set out in single file, under both the setting sun and the rising moon. They were bathed in a dry orange heat, the sun, in descent, catching the mountains, finishing. They walked in silence, Jesse leading the way. A mile down the road, Simon and Nancy began Oms, a guttural rumble at first, and then full-bodied Oms: "Omm, ommm, ommm." Jesse remained quiet. A wave of aloneness swept through him. His separateness—his own doing—speared him with despair. He wanted to run, to disconnect himself from Simon and his nude girl. He wished to swirl into Patty Hearst's life, to yank her from the televised flames that he imagined had consumed her, to save her, to save *it*. You *see*, Molly?

From way in the distance came Dylan. "Like a Rolling Stone." Jesse wrote it off to Simon's grass, but soon it was real, quieting the Oms behind him. They drew closer in their single file, until they were upon it: an empty field, speakers strung for a Saturday-night hoedown, a record on to test the equipment. "Like a Rolling Stone," tinny, like George Harrison in the canyon, metallic, blaring, cruel.

They stopped to listen.

"Isn't that Bob Dylan?" Nancy said.

In his mind, Jesse composed a letter to Molly made up entirely of unconnected pieces of his father's lyrics.

"You know what I'd like? Ice cream," Nancy said.

It became night a little farther down the road. Dylan was a distant star, barely audible, but still wielding influence.

"Om," Simon murmured, almost, Jesse imagined, in parody.

Jesse ran to embrace Molly in the pool, leaving all the others in the wake of his desire. "I'm here at last," he said out loud.

THIS
TIME,
YESTERDAY
MORNING

February 1987

These notes are for me, probably to be discovered by Molly at the bottom of my bottom desk drawer at the start of a new age. Spoken dialogue rings as fiction to me, as in a story or novel. I've always sat removed from my exchanges, reading them while contributing to them. So here, on this complicated morning, I'll dress up a little as a Writer, even though, in the last fourteen months, I have published magazine articles, under my name, on Bette Midler, Stephen Stills, Jesse Barfield of the Toronto Blue Jays, and John "Speak up" Stennis. I'll do the best I can with the truth, despite new paragraphs, semicolons, the folderol of invention.

Annie has a half brother now, Noah Savitt. He was born yesterday just before noon in New York Hospital. He was delivered by Caesarean section, and the first song he heard was (is) "Swingin' Down the Lane" (more later). He is healthy, and looks like a frog. It was snowing heavily during the procedure, just as it was pouring rain as Julia gave birth to Annie. I've got to believe that most babies are delivered during precipitation; except Israeli children. They are parched and crusty children. They are ready to defend before they are able to sit. They seldom dehydrate, and at very early ages consume enormous breakfasts. This is because there is no precipitation during labor and birth. I am confident of this.

Molly, ever so careful at forty, journeyed over to Seventieth and York for stress tests during these last few weeks of pregnancy. I had to drive her there, or taxi her there on three of these (I thought) needless and excessive occasions. I affected monosyllabic behavior in the car or taxi to show displeasure, disapproval—hatred of Molly—but with a very reasonable rap going when I spoke at all. Supportive (though cold), comforting (probably not at all), though I am something of an illusionist, and I do think that very occasionally Molly bought it. But on the other hand, having known her all these years, I am aware that Molly was sometimes faking the buy, for fear I might smack her psychologically, or actually give her a kick or a cuffing. But she is orgasmically truthful, so *let* her fake buy, for the sake of equanimity. But look how goofy this is: a guy in a taxi is selling false attitude; the girl, knowing it is false, is eager to appear as if purchasing. Thus, you have two liars traveling crosstown, getting through it by the skin of their teeth, and as a result, judging the outing a success.

And yet I've got to clarify. Molly and I work very hard at keeping the hoodwinking to a minimum. We are loving antagonists, spewing facts and figures about each other's greasy pretensions. I know that I'm willing to do real business with her *only* after major confessions and self-flagellation on her side. It's then that I'll drip some liquid out that has something to do with truth from the heart. But I won't (can't) budge without Molly turned on self.

An old friend of my father who knew me as a child—a silly woman with a vigorous and fraudulent "love of life"— a mother of six with the millionaire she married, addressed me one day when I was thirteen. "You're demonic," she told me, cheerfully, as we were walking through an apple orchard on a summer day. I, not knowing the meaning of the word, replied: "Thank you, Yvonne." I was so thrilled to be called demonic, thrilled to be called *anything* by this distracted mother of six. I mean, she had time for *me.* She had thought it out, I was demonic, rather than *nothing*, rather than invisible, as Norman thought he was at the end. I told Prissy, Yvonne's eldest daughter, that her mother thought I was demonic. I told her with considerable pride. We were eating sandwiches on a lawn in Quogue. Prissy was sixteen. She said: "Of course you are, that's part of your charm." Those were her exact words, sometime in the summer of 1951. Late in the summer. September. I remember the hay fever.

Is it a part of my charm to drip Molly dry? (I'll tell you this: she can get up off the floor and approach the problem from a different angle. She's a tough girl to keep pinned.)

Let me look up "demonic."

"With evil spirit."

No. Yvonne was wrong. Entirely wrong. People are fearful of my *panic*, because I've packaged it in an innocuous box. But there are those who can hear the ticking inside when they first spot the box on the coffee table. What they experience is a disquieting contradiction. I pose as placid, which poses a threat. Yvonne, others, read demonic for panic. Can you imagine the pose of the thirteen-year-old boy I was? Just a wild thing, clinging to a limb of a Chekhovian maple tree while an electric saw buzzed menacingly, inches from my fingers. Demonic? *It was Yvonne's saw.*

This time, yesterday morning, in all that snow, with *Till*

Eulenspiegel on the radio, I drove Molly over and dropped her off at eight-thirty, and then went on to an interview scheduled at nine (more later). Another routine stress test. Not mother stress, though let me tell you there's got to be a better way, but baby stress: how is the baby doing in the womb. We were having a boy, we knew, though during the amniocentesis months ago, watching on the sonograph screen, I had suddenly blurted out, "Lisa!" I was so sure that Noah was Lisa. Swimming in an early-Bergman black-and-white lake, I saw my second daughter, gliding, turning, swooping. Lisa.

Noah, instead. Molly had been right all along; she was carrying an introspective boy, a boy, she felt, who will want to be left alone to daydream in his room. A very musical boy—considering his grandfather—and probably an intense boy within the introspection. In other words, angry, with temper, like his parents. This had been Molly's view, is Molly's view.

My view was no view at all: Molly is pregnant, let's get through it as best we can. I wanted a girl, like Annie, but even on so grand a topic, I was absent from any real dialogue, or idea. My labor was absenteeism, mindlessness, baseball thoughts, saloonism (hanging out blankly with strangers), nap-ism, absolutely no Rodgers and Hammerstein soul-searching. It was *Molly's* pregnancy. She was married at last, but late in the ball game. We had settled in at once, burdened with a sexual ulterior motive: to impregnate Molly Malick Savitt. We would come together at just the right moment of the month. Then Molly would stand on her head on the bathroom rug for twenty minutes to allow my sperm greater access.

Past and present tense at work here, you notice, and not

without thought. It's what happens. Things get tossed around the now and not-quite-yet of it. Is You Is or Is You Ain't 'Ma Baby.

Molly paraded us to laboratories where we found new terminology for me: low motility. My sperm, lethargic, apparently meandered indifferently up and about Molly. The implication of booze hung heavy in the air. "It has nothing to do with drinking," I said, was forced to say, during ensuing discussions. "It has *everything* to do with drinking," Molly said adamantly. And furthermore, what with this low-motility business, if you, Jesse Savitt, would be *kind* enough to be sexually abstemious on your absolute own (in the silence of your lonely room, that is) for four days and four nights prior to my perfect time, why then . . .

On a beautiful morning in early May, in the office of a doctor named Morgan Morgan, I was placed in a bathroom with a copy of *Playboy*. Molly, around the bend on an examining table, awaited my output. Morgan Morgan's nurse, Melissa, had unknowingly chosen the issue of *Playboy* with my article on steroids in sports, with which I stood, behind closed doors, narcissistically reading from the beginning to the end. I know about the narcissism because: (1) I enjoyed it so terribly much. (2) I caught a quick glimpse of myself in the mirror over the sink that reflected a cheap little grin of pleasure. I hadn't been aware of the grin, so pleased and busy was I with the printed page.

The centerfold was a girl named Randi in whom I had no interest. I called on memory, feeling the pressure of Molly's open-legged impatience down the hall.

Noah was created moments later by Morgan Morgan under a Hopper print in a small gray room.

"I CAN'T SLEEP," Molly said, in the middle of the night, early in her pregnancy. Her urgency assumed that I too was unable to sleep, was lying there in receptive silence, awaiting her remarks.

"Go to sleep," I said, from somewhere.

"I can't."

"Take a phenobarbital."

"I did."

"Take another one."

"I did."

"Go to sleep."

"I can't."

"Have a little Irish whiskey."

"I wish I could."

"Think spiritual thoughts."

"I wish I could."

Molly went through many consecutive nights of not sleeping.

She sought out holistic corners of the city; she purchased mysterious teas and potions; she wept from fatigue, bent over, emitting epileptic garble.

She moved to the living room couch, where she watched the sunrise in tears. What must she have thought of me, asleep, so deeply asleep down the hall, without any *idea* of her pregnancy, with no particular interest in it that she could fathom. The man she married, after fifteen years of broken courting, after several furious fistfights, after long-distance calls stretching all through the night into daybreak, into the morning hours—on one occasion, thirteen hours from New York to Los Angeles, in 1972. This was the man asleep in there. What had taken him so long in Dr. Morgan's office? His drinking, that's what. He'll be fifty years old soon soon soon. Low motility. Needing an *eternity* in Morgan's office. *What have I gotten myself into?*

"Wake up," Molly said, at 5 A.M. one morning.

"I'm awake," I said, having picked up her determination coming down the hall.

"I don't want this baby," Molly said.

Her eyes were swollen from weeping; her voice, husky and glamorous, was informed by night decisions.

"Don't be nuts. Don't be any more nuts than you are," I said.

"I *am* nuts. I've failed you. I've failed the baby."

"That kind of thinking is nuts."

"Is that what you meant by nuts?"

"Of course."

"I don't believe you."

"Molly, what's troubling you is that you have no control over this thing. Take a look at your datebook. All those plans, in *ink,* for *years.* As if the act of writing them down in all that detail would ensure that everyone involved with every item in your very serious datebook would cooperate a hundred percent. No one would get the flu and have to cancel, no one would be subtly insulted by you on the phone a week before and decide to wipe you off your very own agenda. You can't *control* this pregnancy, and in sleep you don't even have a compass. So you're awake, trying to control the air."

No response.

"What do you think?"

"I want to die."

"Let's talk about it at eight."

Molly remained sitting on the side of the king-size bed, far from where I lay. I rose from beneath the covers, from the innards of the bed, and flung myself over Molly, announcing an unscheduled event.

Later, I said, "Some of the best things happen if they're not written down six months earlier."

"The woman who wrote *Childless by Choice* is trying to get pregnant," Molly replied, sipping a holistic potion with a cloying grape flavor.

THIS TIME, YESTERDAY morning.

I drove Molly to another stress test, slowly, very cautiously inching up First Avenue in the snow, slip-sliding away.

We were of neutral cast, unspecific, unterritorial, resolved, for the moment, in a collaborative indifference, not afraid of each other, happy with the outside focus of the snow. We were New Yorkers. We knew this snow. We knew our own minds—how to traverse, how to salvage the hot chocolate of it. We were a part of the earth of the city, had negotiated for so many years the shortcuts through the bluster. Our togetherness was all that accompanied our trip up First Avenue. The fact of it was sufficient.

I dropped Molly off at Seventieth and York, continuing on to an interview with an economist at Ninetieth and Central Park West.

Brahms was on the radio. What did I know of the guy?

I knew a painting of him playing the piano, in Yvonne's husband's living room thirty years ago. Johannes Brahms, who never heard a recording of his music, never spoke on the telephone to a crony, never drove to a stress test, leaving Mrs. Brahms (Gerta, I imagined) at the corner of Seventieth and York. I imagined her wrist tag in the hospital: BRAHMS, GERTA. Her husband's arrival challenges visiting hours. "I'm sorry, Mr. Brahms, but visiting hours were over at eight." Brahms, standing there in a very old overcoat, snow on his hat, his thump thump thump down the hall of the sixth floor vividly masculine and disruptive. A nurse named Tina tells him about the visiting hours. She is impatient and incredulous because it is two-thirty in the morning. "You're far too late, Mr. Brahms." And Brahms leaving, thump thump thump, unfulfilled, Gerta dead asleep in room 614, stirring at the commotion in the hall, but remaining asleep, happy to be away from Brahms, even for only a few days. His clomp at home, his beard, the very *Brahms* of him. Brahms in the bathtub, naked and peculiar, Brahms in pajamas, silent, sober, absent.

I called my service from the economist's living room.

Julia had left a message: call her, urgent.

"Where have you *been?*" she said, hysteria somewhere in her voice.

"What the *fuck* do you mean, *where have I been,*" I said furiously, aware of the economist across the room, a slender homosexual browsing through *USA Today.*

"There's going to be a C-section over there. Molly called. She couldn't find you, where have you *been?*"

"I'm at an *interview.* Where do you *think* I've been!"

"I wouldn't know," she said contemptuously.

The implication was dalliance, her concern through our own marriage.

"I just left her," I said.

"You just left her?"

"I *took* her to the hospital for a stress test."

In the brief silence that followed, I heard Julia grappling with this news, realizing that I had actually been there, not on a dalliance.

I received her disappointment empathically, and let her loose.

"Honey, Julia, what's the story again?"

"Molly thought I might know where you were," she said quietly.

"I told her where I was going to be."

"Well, she didn't know, didn't remember. She thought I could find you. The baby's coming by Caesarean. The test showed some fetal discomfort, so they thought it best to go in and get it."

"When?"

"Now."

"You OK?"

"I'm OK."

FETAL DISCOMFORT. WHAT could that mean? The umbilical cord wrapped around Noah improperly, or some psychological development: Noah angry, pissed off, bleeping the monitor, creating fetal distress.

Molly had called Julia, knowing that Julia was handy on the telephone, that she would track me down quickly. Julia had often said: "I'm only four phone calls away from reaching anyone in the world." And she had extended friendship to Molly, without a rule book in her hand.

I had wanted to use the economist's phone to show off a busy schedule, a service-calling life in the city, even in a snowstorm, even at nine in the morning.

Molly was being prepared for surgery in the very room in which Julia, five years ago, had experienced labor. Arnold Miller was on the scene again, retained by the common father and his second wife.

"There were indications of some distress," he told me in the hall. "I think it's sound to end the pregnancy," he said. "There are very few risks here," he went on.

Dr. Miller was a shy man with evasive eyes that were often cast down (Molly had called it "fluttering"). He addressed the floor with a touch of a smile. His eyes would slide up at the end of whatever it was he was saying, offering, hoping for, a conclusion, in a business that held no solid endings, just questions through the days and nights, questions on the phone, questions in the mail. Dr. Arnold Miller was up against it, had chosen to be up against it. He would never be left in peace—he was a father of four himself, *think* of the questions in his home.

Molly alone had filled his weeks with shotgun problems, outside of his other patients, outside of his own four children, and his wife, named Loretta (I had found this out). Now, here was Miller, on the delivery floor on a snowy day, faced with yet another fetal distress, a soggy father with a mouth filled with questions of his own, and a woman, trembling in fear, an IV already attached.

I thought to humor Molly, as silent tears spoke for her terror.

"Remember that tutor of mine I told you about? Max? He made a terrible mistake once." I waited for Molly's full attention.

"Max was on a panel of some kind," I continued when I felt Molly was with me, "and one of the other guys was a new black professor at Max's college, who told the group that he had been born Caesarean. I don't know why he told the group this, but he did.

"Max wanted to show the black guy they had something in common, and with much enthusiasm he said, 'What a coincidence. *I* was born Caucasian!'"

Molly laughed, muffling herself, not wanting to disturb the IV, or Noah.

"Our baby has had a rich and full pregnancy to work

with," I said. "This last trimester was real serene. You've got nothing to worry about." I took Molly's hand. "He was due this Friday, today is Tuesday. That doesn't spell bad news to me."

"I know," Molly said.

"Fifteen years, honey, and here we are. And it's snowing, and it's all cozy in here. Miller was *in* the *hospital,* for Christ's sake. Now isn't that a good omen?"

"Yes," Molly said softly.

During the last few moments of Molly's preparation, I wandered down the hall to look around.

The C-section operating room was twice the size of the room in which Annie had been born, a room even now in use. The door was slightly ajar. I could see a woman's belly. It looked so quiet in there, where Annie had come, where Julia had lain. Even on the operating table Julia had been gracious, social.

I changed to surgical attire in the same walk-in closet I'd used in 1982. Mask, paper slippers, like everyone else on the floor. I was dressed in green when I went back to Molly.

"It's now," Molly said, her tears gone away.

"Should you be sleepy with medication?" I asked.

"I'm awake sleepy," she said.

I went with her. The hospital allowed it. A sheet was pulled high, a screen before her, preventing her from viewing the surroundings.

"My God," I said as we entered the operating room, "do *all* C-section rooms have pianos?"

Arnold Miller thought that was funny. It was a question he had never heard, easy to answer. He would remember this one.

"A couple," he replied.

"A piano?" Molly said vaguely.

"Only an upright," I said. "A Yamaha."

"That's not possible, is it?"

"No," I said, "but it's an idea whose time has come."

I sat right with her, the sheet obscuring the procedure, and held her arm.

"I feel pressure," Molly said. Her arms were spread wide, strapped down.

"Pressure," she said again.

"It's a small incision," I said. "They've got to maneuver the baby."

"That's right," Miller said, from the other side of the sheet.

Unaccountably, I thought of the frightened eyes of the pitcher Calvin Schiraldi. I thought of my father. "Marry Molly," he had advised, on Cape Cod, so long ago. There had been a gray summer light behind him, turning to black as a storm rolled in. He had been standing in front of a fireplace with a log in his arms, facing me. "Marry Molly."

"Marry Molly," I said.

She knew the source, but didn't respond.

I was sitting at Molly's side, my head above hers. Our eyes were locked at the moment of Noah's first cry. Our own tears came at once, our eyes securely attached.

"Yes," I kept saying to Molly. "Yes."

Noah was hustled across the room for testing. I watched, programmed by Molly for the worst. In her fourth month a mouse had scooted across the kitchen floor. Molly *knew* that the result would be toxoplasmosis and the inevitable retardation of her child. "You can't get *rid* of mouse droppings," she had said.

In her sixth month, in a taxi, she had said: "I know my fate."

"What is your fate," I had said.

223

"Premature detachment of the placenta. I know it."

"It's called placenta primavera," I had said.

In her seventh month, in the middle of the night, she had said: "I know my fate."

"What is your fate."

"My adrenaline will drown the baby. I know it."

In her eighth month, on Christmas morning, she had said: "The baby will come out damaged because my body couldn't possibly be a source of nurturing. What do *I* know from nurturing?"

And the phenobarbitals. And the three or four cigarettes in the nine months. And the sleepless nights. And the slipping on the stairs one day. Surely the baby would be born deaf, or a drug addict, or bizarre.

In one minute, Noah was pronounced fit. He was handed to me wrapped in soft material. He resembled no one. He was quiet and dumbfounded.

I held him up for his mother to see. Molly's eyes were dry. She studied, more than caressed, her son.

"He's perfect," I told her. "He's got a perfect Apgar score. A ten, right off the bat."

"Gosh," Molly said, and only that.

"Noah," I said, into Noah's faceless face.

"Sing to him," Molly said.

Immediately I did so: "When the moon is on the wane / Still I'm waiting all in vain / Should be swingin' down the lane / With you."

I know nothing about "Swingin' Down the Lane." I don't know who wrote it, I don't know where it came from. But it's been out there.

Molly had time left on the table; I had taken a glimpse of Dr. Arnold Miller's mess. We stayed for a half hour, swingin' down the lane. Molly's arms trembled, still held in straps.

"Do you think I'll be OK with Noah?" Molly asked, wincing at the discomfort of repair.

"There's no doubt in my mind," I told her, resting my hand on her left arm.

"And he's not blind," she asked.

"No," I said.

"How do they know absolutely."

"They tested him right over there. I saw them do it."

"And he's not injured?"

"No. Look," I said, again holding Noah for his mother to see.

We waited without talking for a little while.

"Why don't you sing him a song by your father," Molly finally said.

I held Noah close to me.

"OK, boy, now listen to this," I said, my face inches from his face. "I've got an absolutely great song for you. You'll *love* it. It's a cowboy kind of song."

And I sang:

"Over the Purple Hills
Far away, far far away
There's a field and a stream
And a truth to the dream
For the rider who canters these hills at dawn
It's the mission he's on
It's the love in his song
And the chance that he's willing to take if he's wrong
Over the Purple Hills."

WAITING
WEEPING

Norman flying home from Los Angeles, or from Boston, or from London. Jesse waiting, as he is now, for a glimpse, that first glimpse, Norman entering customs, Jesse above, glass-enclosed, trying to catch his father's eye, waving. Daddy! Sorrow, and some kind of crying. Waiting weeping. Norman, emerging from an airport tube, or off a DC-6, squinting in whatever light there was years ago. Norman in his blue suit, wearing his black shoes, carrying a briefcase that implies order. In truth, Norman's papers are in kitchen cabinets and behind leather chairs. In that briefcase: jottings on music paper, obit clippings, phone bills—notices of disconnection—half a Mounds bar, *Variety*, a dozen sharpened pencils, loose ear Flents, nose drops, a Xerox of a magazine piece by Jesse.

Jesse has always waited, his car in the lot at Kennedy or La Guardia. He has waited for his dad, seeing only his dad in the middle of his mind, even as he has drifted through the airport cafeteria, scavenging for left-behind French fries or slices of pickle.

Norman Savitt is coming home, back, white-haired these

days, cautious, exhibiting discomfort with each elderly step, not hunched or classically aged; rather, filled with terror of fast vehicles, horn blowing, elevators, telephones, insomnia, thunder, restaurant food, friends dying, as is the case now—Bert Skyler in Los Angeles, a friend from the thirties, a public relations guy around the theater who kept in touch.

Jesse waits by the metal detector, peering down the long carpeted tube for the sight of this most wondrous of men, eighty-four years old next Tuesday—there will be a reception upstairs at Sardi's. Vincent Sardi was once a dapper host, ubiquitous in his joint, sailing behind Leonard Lyons. His guard is still up, though his fatigue is palpable. He is giving Norman Savitt a reception, smack in the teeth of the end of Reagan's second campaign. "Why *not* election night?" Norman has reasoned. "Kern and Hammerstein opened *Music in the Air* on the night of FDR's first plurality."

Five o'clock in the afternoon on a Friday. That means a long drive into the city, heavy traffic, a crawl over the Triborough Bridge, Norman filled with haunting stories of death and failure, of Bert Skyler's funeral, of friendships that died years before Skyler and were awakened for Bert's one slim moment at noontime in Beverly Hills. All of Skyler's phone calls since 1933 had, in that hour, come to fruition.

Everybody had always taken Bert's calls. Everybody liked Bert Skyler. He was something of a cartoonist, scrawling little faces on the bottom of his publicity stuff, little personal faces, caricatures. There were whispers of truth in those drawings, unmalicious info from the pen of an engaging artiste, comfortable in the company of Irving Lazar or Irwin Shaw or Dana Andrews—it was thought that Skyler had put Andrews on the wagon. "Dana put himself on the wagon," Bert had always said, when it had come up.

Skyler, ingratiating to the end, had expired in his very own bed without a whimper of alarm, antagonizing no one with hospitals and telegrams and items in the press. A modest conclusion, deserving of Norman's attendance.

THE "ARRIVAL" SCREEN has said "Landing" for a half hour, then "Landed," but it is a busy time of day and there are no gates available. Another half hour for Jesse to peer down the tube, waiting for the sight of the familiar white head, taking its own sweet time, traversing the corridor with trepidation, filled with imagined bad news to be imparted in Jesse's Datsun in a traffic jam.

This time, Norman, returning from an actual funeral, is rightfully in possession of gloomy material. Coming off the road with a show, or home from London after a theater catch-up, Norman would start off festively, only to languish in tragedy by Ninety-sixth and Lexington. This time, Jesse is expecting no fun at all. Surely, Beverly Hills had poked at the slumbering Norman Savitt with a stick, awakening his memory, igniting his sorrows. Jesse expects no diamonds in the dirt, despite all of Bert Skyler's caricatures, and friendly missiles of invitation delivered by hand in any city in the world. At the funeral, Jesse imagines, awash in the eulogies of Johnny Green and Joe Mankiewicz, Norman must have focused on his own misadventures, wrong turns way back then, financial woes when the world saw him as wealthy, caught in the pose of abundance, writing songs for mirthless movies starring Fernando Lamas, placing phone calls to Carol in the East. Her hospital bills had wiped Norman out. She said she'd be well soon, by his side in California, to join him in their house at Lomitas and Crescent—$35,000 in

1941, purchased from Ann Sothern, worth what now? A block south of the Beverly Hills Hotel? But in 1946, when Norman sold it, he had walked away with $75,000, thinking himself a financial genius.

Finally comes the cavalcade of disembarkers, swooshing down the tube toward Jesse, dragging their paraphernalia, racing forward with the special urgency peculiar to released passengers. Some find their chauffeurs, men holding signs high above their heads: STEIN, MILLER, SLATNICK.

Even the stewardesses, their bags on wheels, beat Norman out.

Jesse spends a minute wondering if he's gotten it right: flight number, arrival time, airport. Everything checks out.

And there he is.

The word "caboose" occurs to Jesse.

He is alone on the red carpet, carrying only an overcoat, Jesse not yet in his view. His legs hurt. Jesse had bought him a stationary bicycle, and had placed it in Norman's study. It has remained riderless, very much, Jesse imagines, like the horse at JFK's funeral.

"Daddy!" he finally shouts. "Were you on a backup plane?"

Jesse embraces his father. They are on those terms.

"How was it?"

"There were a lot of people I remembered," Norman says. "I'm glad I went."

"You must have been greeted warmly," Jesse says, taking his father by the arm.

"After a fashion." Norman walks with his son toward the baggage area.

"What do you mean, 'after a fashion.' "

"Well, it wasn't really *my* event," Norman says. "The focus was on Bert."

"Yes, but still."

"My event . . ."

"What about your event."

"I got a letter from Bert only about a week ago. Just Hollywood talk. About a week ago."

"Things move fast," Jesse says, steering his father down a flight of stairs.

"Do you know that after all this time I'm not sure if things are too long or too short, or too fast or too slow. The answers just aren't there." Norman smiles at Jesse.

"That's good for me to know," Jesse says. "It'll save me a lot of work mulling it over."

"You're a muller. There'll be no avoiding it," Norman says.

"But if the evidence is inconclusive all the way into your eighties, then what good is a proper work ethic along the way?" Jesse muses.

"The evidence isn't inconclusive to one and all, I suppose," Norman says. "There are those who find answers with what *they* consider factual stuff."

"What's better?" Jesse asks, "not having a clue, or being absolutely sure."

"There you go again," Norman says with a laugh.

"Where do I go again," Jesse asks.

"Prolonging the undebatable."

"Come on now, Norman Savitt, everything's debatable."

"That's open to question, don't you think?"

IN THE CAR Norman is chatty at first.

"I took a drive through Beverly Hills," he is saying. "My *God,* what little change there. I mean between Sunset and

Santa Monica. Our house, just like it was. Everything. Your school on Rexford. No signal lights anywhere. And the alleys. Do you have any recollection of the crescent trees on Crescent Drive?"

"Yes," Jesse says. "They were sticky, weren't they? Like when you get cotton candy on your wrist."

"Do you remember that they were all found to be diseased, and the entire street, the whole length of Crescent Drive, was altered forever. All those trees were taken out, and new ones were planted. Just after the war. Come to think of it, maybe 1943 or 1944."

"I was through there a year ago with Julia," Jesse says. "You're right. Not a trace of change."

"Julia," Norman says, asking his question.

"I don't see us coming back together," Jesse says. "And I can't point a finger at her. She and I, the *package,* is a special kind of friendship, not a marriage. It's a friendship of unentangling devotion."

"Annie," Norman says, asking again.

"Julia and I have spoken with several shrinks. They have all said, split now, before Annie knows the difference. She's just two. We didn't say we were separated. We didn't want to color their advice. But it does seem right, doesn't it?" Jesse, driving, glances at his father.

"Julia is so spirited," Norman says.

"Yes," Jesse says.

They fall into silence for a while.

Traffic on the bridge is moving along. At the toll, Jesse looks at his father and finds that Norman is asleep. Jesse thinks this is unusual. Norman, always a jumpy passenger, has never allowed himself to drift off in any vehicle.

With his eyes closed, Norman appears older. In the absence of his youthful blue eyes, his face has collapsed a bit, hinting at his skeleton.

"Daddy," Jesse says, testing his father's aliveness, as he had often tested his daughter's, creeping up by the crib when Annie was an infant to inspect the testimony of her breathing.

Norman's eyes shoot open defensively. It takes him a second or two to gather his bearings.

Jesse imagines that his father had been far away, up in an attic, filled, perhaps, with Playbills and 78s and clothes that Jesse's mother had worn. Maybe a red cashmere sweater that Jesse now recalls as he circles onto the FDR Drive. His mother's red sweater at the foot of her bed, like a folded quilt.

"Short trip," Norman says, rolling down the window to allow a warm November breeze into the car.

"You slept most of the way. Are you OK?" Jesse asks.

"I'm tired."

"That's to be expected, isn't it? All that flying in forty-eight hours."

"It was important to go," Norman says. "It was kind of like an overall ending."

"You mean the funeral."

"More generally, for me, I guess. It was a look at a past point, when you were what? Five? Six?"

"You don't have to work me in on *my* account," Jesse says with a laugh.

"Your account is my account."

"So I got a free ride."

"You could say that."

"But you say an overall ending."

"Well, I meant, it's not likely to happen again."

"You mean the war? Crescent Drive? The trees?"

Jesse rests his hand on Norman's knee, trying to steer him away from what he thinks his father really means.

"All of it," Norman says. "It was of a period."

"Everything is. Fractions of seconds are periods."

"What are you trying to say?" Norman asks seriously.

"What I'm trying to say is: hold no regrets. Comprenez-vous?"

"Well, now that you put it like that," Norman says, resting his hand on his son's for a moment.

"I mean it," Jesse says.

"I know," Norman says, comfortably withdrawing his hand. "You're a serious boy."

NORMAN LIKES HIS apartment dark. Though it overlooks Fifth Avenue from the fourth floor, the curtains are seldom open, and only the study light burns regularly. Jesse feels a Dickensian muskiness as he helps his father return.

"Judging by this place, you wouldn't exactly be considered a merry prankster," Jesse says, laying his father's suitcase on the bed.

"On the other hand, what you see could be the prank," Norman replies, with a nice droll look about him, a poker face, only occasionally available in him. Jesse feels that his father's wit has more to do with mental banana peels than with twisty cynicism or rambunctious irony, though on these last two counts Jesse has noticed Norman take a greater interest in the possibilities. When did Norman catch on at all? Maybe in his seventies, Jesse thinks, having run out of things to do.

"You want a drink?" Jesse asks, going into the kitchen for ice.

"I'd like a ginger ale," Norman replies from the living room, leafing through what little mail has accumulated.

"Someday, maybe you'll *have* a drink, right?" Jesse yells, from the refrigerator.

Norman makes no reply.

When Jesse returns with two glasses, his father drops anchor on a thorny issue.

"You know what I think about your drinking," he says, affecting no inflection that might inflame his son.

"You say 'your drinking' as if it were an entity," Jesse says. "As if we were a twosome."

"You are, aren't you?" Norman says, slowly sitting down in his favorite black leather chair.

"Other people drink without entity. Why am I singled out?"

"I've always told you this, Jesse. You have always consumed too much liquor for my taste."

"Even the word 'liquor' is clinical out of you. Try 'Scotch.'"

"What about the afternoon vodkas?"

"Try booze, and the vodka is singular. Don't moisten the ball."

"What?"

"Don't fool with the facts. Vodka is singular, if that, and you know it. What's your beef?" Jesse stands in front of his father, holding his drink.

"My boy, I have no beef. I just want to see you in the best of health."

"Do I look sick?" Jesse asks, his dander up a bit.

"Of course not," Norman says.

"Well, then, what's the issue?"

"Don't make a mountain out of a molehill."

"Oh, I see," Jesse says, keeping it going. "My entity is now a molehill. All in one minute."

"You've always been very strong like that," Norman says reflectively. "I don't know if it's a good or a bad thing."

"What is a good or a bad thing?" Jesse asks, understanding, wishing for an unnagging satisfaction.

"Your ability to reason critics down to mush," Norman says, choosing his words carefully.

"I hadn't noticed that you were being critical," Jesse says, taking a seat on the sofa.

"Well, you're very talented anyway," Norman says, hoping to conclude.

"Haven't you ever thought to have a drink?" Jesse continues, without any formal strategy in mind.

"I've had many drinks," Norman says.

"All that Trader Vic's crap. Rum and sugar and piss," Jesse says.

"Do you think it's a masculine characteristic to drink whiskey?" Norman asks, appearing interested in the flow of events.

"You know, that's a good question," Jesse replies. "I suppose there's something to it. It's not limited to journalists, obviously. Or journalism, my field. Though it's in the blood, I suppose, in a not feminine way."

"But what about all those women reporters out there these days?" Norman asks, sliding his leather chair into a more deeply reclining position.

"I'm ambivalent about them, if the truth be known," Jesse says, taking a sip of his Scotch and soda. "There's an awful lot of drinking and aggression in this new pack."

"Generally, do you get along with the other people?"

"It's not as if I'm on a newspaper where there's a consistent crowd I've got to deal with. I'm all over the place. Sure. Sure, I get along. I get along within the industry. People respect me, so I start off pretty well in a new setting."

Jesse pauses, thinking that his father is no longer unrelenting. Norman's positions, like the one on the table, were, for years, tenacious. Why doesn't Jesse *really* get along in the industry? What about behavior? What about drinking? *I'm doing the best I can,* Dad. But Norman would step backstage after such a curtain line to continue the show: What does *best* mean? How can you be *sure* you're doing it? All of this with Jesse standing in front of the mirror removing his makeup. *I'm doing the best I can.* Curtain. And now some guy's in the dressing-room doorway, unconvinced.

But not *this* Norman Savitt. Not this now eighty-four-year-old man, back from Bert Skyler's funeral. Not even the N. Savitt of three or four years ago. Benign acceptance set in at about that time. The only thing left is to get Norman's grimy hands off Jesse's sacred bottle.

"What time is it?" Norman suddenly wants to know.

Jesse tells him, and says that he's got to go.

"What about you coming with me to the party Tuesday?" Norman asks.

"I *am* coming," Jesse says. "And Julia too."

"I meant *with* me," Norman says, beginning to struggle out of his immense leather chair to walk his son to the door.

"Would you like that? Sure. Of course," Jesse says, rearranging Julia in his mind.

"Julia could meet you there," Norman says.

"That's easy. No problemo. You and I will go together."

Jesse puts his arms around his father, creating a nice hug. "Maybe you won't be totally abstemious at your own affair," Jesse says, into his father's neck.

"I'll have a nip."

"I guess what you think is, with me it's nip and tuck."

"I've never thought it was that crucial. I just want to know you're at your best."

"Maybe you'll play some of your songs at the party," Jesse says at the elevator.

"People aren't much interested anymore," Norman says. "Only Bert Skyler, and look what happened to him."

JESSE WAITS DOUBLE-PARKED in front of his father's building. It is six in the evening; Norman was due downstairs at a quarter of six.

Jesse gets out of the car and passes under the awning and into the lobby, asking the doorman to ring upstairs. Jesse is told that Mr. Savitt will be down in a minute.

Jesse goes back to the car, and sits at the wheel with the motor running.

It is an unusually balmy night, distinctly humid, with the threat of a thundershower. Jesse considers turning on the air conditioner, but knows it would drown the Bach on the radio with static. The two elements in the car are separated, he imagines, by a fragile membrane, translucent, vulnerable to exertion, unrepairable. (To Jesse, most things are unrepairable. Most things must be taken into some kind of shop east of York Avenue in the Seventies to be worked on and worked on. Or other things must be taken into some kind of store west of Eleventh Avenue in the Fifties to be replaced.)

Jesse stays with the music, which has become *Peter and the Wolf,* narrated by David Bowie. Peter's soaring theme, its subdued entrance and its vivid growth, stirs him. He cries out suddenly, surprising himself: "Oh mama!"

Lost in the music, Jesse, who had planned to observe his father as he came through the innards of the lobby, and out under the awning, and around to the passenger door, is startled when that door is carefully opened. Almost delicately, Norman finds his seat, sliding slowly in next to Jesse, with a grave countenance.

"What's the matter?" Jesse asks.

"I'm not up to snuff this evening," Norman says.

He is wearing a gray suit, an orange tie with a dark blue shirt.

"You look a little tired," Jesse says with concern.

"Actually, I just got up," Norman says. "I was napping. I'll be OK."

"The party will be right up your alley. You'll play the piano, you'll see some friends. What could be so bad?"

"Nothing's bad," Norman says. "I wish I felt better, that's all."

"Well, you will. You will."

"I've got to get myself up for it," Norman says as Jesse pulls into the flow of Fifth Avenue traffic.

"You always do," Jesse says.

"It's such a job," Norman says. "Would you turn off the radio?"

"No problemo," Jesse says.

They ride downtown together in silence.

At Forty-eighth Street, they are held up briefly by construction.

"Damn it," Norman says, uncharacteristically.

"It's just traffic, Papa," Jesse says.

"We're already late," Norman says.

Jesse experiences a wave of guilt: late. Himself to blame. But not at all. Norman wasn't accusing.

In his relief, Jesse rests his hand on his father's knee.

"It's only a party," Jesse says soothingly.

Jesse parks on Forty-third between Sixth and Broadway.

"It's not seven o'clock yet," his father warns ominously.

"I like our chances," Jesse says.

On the street Norman is slower than ever. Jesse, his arm around his father's back, accommodates the pace.

"Is it raining?" Norman says, trying to find the sky.

"It's misting," Jesse says. "You know November, don't you? You were born in November."

"Damn it, I should have brought an umbrella."

"It's only a mist, like a fog. Take it easy."

"I *am* taking it easy," Norman insists.

Vincent Sardi greets them with professional enthusiasm.

Norman takes the stairs up to the second floor with an alacrity designed, Jesse knows, to fool the populace.

On the way up, Jesse, behind his father and in front of Sardi, admires his father's strength, the determined push of his prolongation. Jesse thinks that it's carried off by people of unusual courage: an elderly singer slipping past the vowel by scurrying to the "v" of "love" on a high F; the knuckleballer, still in there at fifty, toughing it out. Norman Savitt, neither singer nor pitcher, can call on only his eyes—milk-blue eyes with youth at the center. He understands that he can persevere, causing only one or two skeptical murmurs from the audience.

Now, at the top of the stairs, glancing back at his son for last-minute support, Norman is prepared. With love, Jesse extends his hand, touching his father's fingertips.

DURING THE PARTY, Jesse sticks by his father's side. There isn't a big crowd, but all have been friends through the years.

"You look fifty, Norman."

"We gotta do a show, you and I."

"I saw you at Bert Skyler's funeral, but it was too jammed to get to you."

"Norman, you are a festival of pleasure." This from Julia. She has turned up in a gay red dress, and with shorter hair than Jesse can ever recall, having been around her since 1979. At the moment, Julia and Jesse have lawyers on telephones. No one is contesting a thing, but the air is charged, though graced in public with civility. Jesse kisses Julia on the cheek, a new kind of kiss, developed over the last year: a dry, neutral wisp of a thing, no more than a punctuation mark of hello.

Vincent Sardi has supplied Dom Perignon. Julia holds a glass in each hand. One is for Norman.

"Come on now, spirit of birthday futures, this one's for you," she says, cramming a slender glass into Norman's indecision.

There is an upright piano in a corner. Norman is at it after only a sip or two of champagne.

His melodies capture the party. Everyone has a view of him. Everyone knows "On the Other Hand," "I'm Part of You," "Over the Purple Hills."

Jesse sees that his father is perspiring. He moves to the piano bench, and, with a paper napkin, dabs at his father's forehead.

Norman, absorbed, pays no attention. He fields requests, suggests other composers' songs.

"Rodgers," he says. "How about some Rodgers!"

Vincent Sardi, in the background, beams affectionately.

Jesse notices that Julia and Arlene Francis are laughing together. They are standing near Sardi by the top of the stairs.

For a moment Jesse can't recall Julia's maiden name. He whispers his daughter's name over and over again. "Annie, Annie, Annie." He discovers that Julia's maiden name is Oppenheimer. He had lost it for only a second or two, and disregards the incident.

Norman sits at the piano for an hour. His singing voice, suggesting Fred Astaire's, is youthful and articulate.

The heat, for there is no air conditioning on this November evening, has begun to cause discomfort. People begin to drift away, saying their good-nights. Julia is gracious at the door, an instinctive hostess, the last celebrating member of the family.

Others remain for more champagne, surrounding Norman, now seated on a chair in a far corner of the room. He has loosened his tie. To Jesse, he appears weary.

"What a success!" Julia says to Vincent Sardi somewhat later.

"My dear man," Norman tells Sardi, grasping his arm, "you were so generous to do this. It was so unnecessary."

"Oh, but it *was* necessary," Julia says merrily. And then to one and all: "It was a happening, don't you agree?"

———————

THE NIGHT IS heavy, but the rain has held off.

Jesse walks Norman slowly back to the car.

"Oh, Jesse boy, I don't feel so hot," Norman says, his face wet with perspiration.

"Maybe it was the champagne," Jesse says. "You're not used to anything stronger than Diet Seven-Up."

"Where is your mother?" Norman suddenly asks.

"What?" Jesse says.

"Is it ten o'clock yet?" Norman asks.

"It's ten-fifteen, and my mother is with Bert Skyler, and I've got a feeling they're playing backgammon."

"I don't understand you sometimes," Norman says in a very soft voice.

"What do you expect me to say?"

"What?"

"I thought it was a nice party. You played wonderfully."

"Jesse boy, I've got to stop here. Just for a minute, that's all."

They had crossed Times Square, made their way down Forty-fourth Street, and were now at the corner of Forty-third and Sixth.

"Take it easy," Jesse says, his arm around his father.

"Let me rest for a moment," Norman says, trying to catch his breath.

Norman manages a sitting position at the curb, his feet on the grating of the gutter.

Jesse slides down beside him, wiping his father's brow with the palm of his right hand.

"Why did you ask me about my mother?" Jesse says, his arm around his father's neck.

"I lost my composure for a moment," Norman says, his forearms on his legs, his head bent low.

"You should have gotten married again, you know."

"Tell me to whom," Norman says with a tough chuckle.

To whom, Jesse wonders.

There had been a woman related to Walter Annenberg; or the lead in one of Norman's shows; or Lois Hayes, free between marriages to two lawyers, a woman with close ties to Jesse's mother. Norman Savitt had not staggered through these thirty-five years unaccompanied. And yet here he was at Forty-third and Sixth on the evening of his eighty-fourth birthday with his only living relative mopping up the sweat of his father's aloneness with his fingers.

"See the car?" Jesse says, after about five minutes. "It's just over there, just across the avenue."

"OK, OK, here we go," Norman says, gathering as much strength as possible.

Jesse helps his father to his feet.

With extra care they cross Sixth, and maneuver themselves to Jesse's Datsun.

Jesse uses the air conditioner on the way up Madison.

"How are you doin'?" he asks his father, after a moment or so of silence.

"Jesse boy, Jesse boy." Norman shakes his head, saying no, saying no.

"You want to see Berkowitz in the morning?"

"I don't need a doctor. Honestly. He'll tell me it's humid, the seasons are changing. He'll tell me I'm an old man."

"You're *not* an old man," Jesse says.

"I'm old and invisible," Norman says weakly.

"What do you mean by 'invisible'?" Jesse asks. "Do you mean you're not a hit show? Do you mean you're not Bruce Springsteen? I can imagine you at a stadium, Giant Stadium, say. 'Ladies and gentlemen, Norman Savitt!' And you'd come out, dressed like Springsteen—sleeveless, blue jeans, rolling your own piano out. It's on wheels, you dig? The place is jammed with seventy-two thousand people. You sit down on the piano bench, aware that Columbia Records is making an album, aware that a crew of thirty is shooting an MTV video, that clips will be shown later on Roger Grimsby's news, that the *Times* has two guys there. *Two fuckin' guys.* And when you start to play and sing 'Over the Purple Hills' the fuckin' place goes crazy. I mean *crazy!*

"Norman Savitt, face it: there's a new language in the world, just like the way you came along with a new language once upon a time. Language moves at the speed of sound. There are very few people whose imaginations are so strong, so fresh with originality, so alive with the truth, that they push to the limits of the speed of sound, and then break through, in one thrilling moment, so that their language bursts and scatters into fireworks in the sky, and slowly

246

drifts to earth as a permanent part of the soil. *From then on,* however language changes, it will always take with it bits and pieces of those sound-bursting fireworks. You, my dearest daddy, are one of the very few people who flamed the sky with such a light. And you're not even a genius. But that's what you did, you know. And this is not hyperbole. What you've got to do now is lean back and watch the language go by. You'll see your hand in it. The trouble is, you're wasting time wanting to be Springsteen. *Now* is the hour to enjoy the reruns."

Norman makes no reply, except to close his eyes.

Jesse imagines that his father is warding him off: all this talk and where is it leading?

The eyelids drop over the little seas of blue. Even in his fatigue, the muscles in Norman's face are tight, defending, unacquiescent. The sweat? Pretend it isn't happening, suggests the sitting statue of Norman Savitt. Besides, he is saying, my head's in the sand, so you can't see a thing anyway.

Jesse lets the car idle in front of Norman's building to keep the air conditioner on.

"I've got to go up now," Norman says.

"You want me to go with you?" Jesse asks.

"I'm fine," Norman replies. He pats his son's knee.

"I'll take you to Berkowitz in the morning, if you want to go," Jesse says.

"All I need is some sleep."

"Are you sleeping well, or poorly, or what?"

"Spasmodically," Norman says.

"We all go through that," Jesse says, dabbing at his father's forehead one more time.

"How are you fixed for money?" Norman suddenly asks.

"Not great, not lousy. A lot depends on the outcome with Julia."

"She's loaded, isn't she?"

"Yes, but there's Annie."

"If you're short, you know . . ."

"I've always known," Jesse says.

"Are you going to be out of town at all? In the immediate future?"

"No."

"Good."

"Why?"

"I need you, that's all."

"I'm always there."

"Don't forget your old dad."

"Don't go sentimental on me."

"I wasn't being sentimental."

"I know. I didn't mean it in any critical way."

Jesse kisses his father's wet cheek. "Write me a song," Jesse says.

"I've got some absolutely wonderful tunes, you know, that you've never heard." Norman's eyes are wide open with a quick enthusiasm.

"I'd love to hear them."

"I'm still active, you know," Norman says, nodding yes. Nodding yes.

"Doesn't surprise me," Jesse says.

"Well, here I go." Norman takes a big breath of air.

"There you go," Jesse says, holding his father's hand for a moment.

Long after Norman has disappeared inside his building, Jesse lingers in front of it, waiting for a light in any one of Norman's windows.

After twenty minutes, with no sign of Norman's return to the fourth floor, no study light, no bathroom light behind the translucent glass of the corner window, Jesse switches off the motor, turns on the blinkers, locks the car.

In the elevator, he is suddenly faced with the image of his father's fingers resting on a keyboard. They appear, like a miracle, on the wood paneling of the closed door.